the YEAR of the BEASTS

the Year of the BEASTS

CECIL CASTELLUCCI
ILLUSTRATED BY NATE POWELL

ROARING BROOK PRESS
NEW YORK

This book was written in part with a fellowship from the MacDowell Colony.

Library of Congress Cataloging-in-Publication Data

Castellucci, Cecil 1969–
    The year of the beasts / Cecil Castellucci ; illustrated by Nate Powell. — 1st ed.
      p. cm.
    Summary: Fifteen-year-old Tessa tries to be happy when her crush, Charlie, falls for her
younger sister, Lulu, and it becomes easier after she begins a secret relationship with Jasper,
a social outcast who lives next door to Tessa's best friend. Alternate chapters are in graphic
novel form.
    ISBN 978-1-59643-686-2
[1. Dating (Social customs)—Fiction.   2. Sisters—Fiction.   3. Secrets—Fiction.
4. Best friends—Fiction.   5. Friendship—Fiction.]   I. Powell, Nate, ill.   II. Title.
    PZ7.C26865Ye 2012
    [Fic]—dc23

                                                                                2011031727

Roaring Brook Press books are available for special promotions and premiums.
For details contact: Director of Special Markets, Holtzbrinck Publishers.

First edition 2012
Book design by Colleen AF Venable
Printed in the United States of America

10 9 8 7 6 5 4 3 2 1

To brave friends who
do not once turn to stone

chapter one

They rolled into town in the middle of the day: large covered wagons and flatbed trucks hauling disassembled rides that looked like futuristic dinosaur bones. They settled over by the highway, by the river, near the empty muddy brown field and planted themselves. Two days later, sawdust, lights, and swinging rides that screamed against the sky sprouted.

It didn't matter where you were when the carnival arrived, everyone heard it beckon. The air filled with a music that lulled each person to a dreamy calm and seemed to come from a time when life was better. It was hard to believe that a time like that ever existed—safer, quainter, quieter times—but the music made everyone believe. People hummed the tune that reached through the rows of houses and rolled all the way back down to the river like a low fog. It made a person crave corn dogs and cotton candy.

It came once a year for a weekend in June, announcing to all that summer had officially begun. This year was no different than any other. The carnival would open on Friday night, and everyone in town had plans to go.

Tessa and Lulu were no exception. Last year the two sisters had worn matching sundresses and eggshell-colored sweaters—and they had gone with the burden of their parents hovering over them, making them squirm with embarrassment each time they saw someone from school. Accompanied by their parents, they had felt like babies, and, even worse, their mom's sleeve tattoos and their dad's long hair and piercings could have been an attraction at such a place once upon a time. Last year, Tessa and Lulu were not free to try every single ride, brave the curiosity sideshow tent, get lost in the crowds, or win a tiny stuffed banana without help from their father.

But this year was different. This year, Tessa was old enough to go alone. The week the trucks arrived, the two sisters were sent into a tizzy.

"Did you see them rolling into town?" Tessa asked, hoping to one-up her sister.

"No," Lulu said.

"I did," Tessa said. "Guess I'm lucky!"

"Guess you are," Lulu said and tried to not sound too disappointed. But Tessa could tell she was. She wore the sadness on her face all through dinner.

Everyone at her school agreed that Tessa was officially the girl who saw the trucks first that year. Everyone said that was a sign of luck. In fact, it *was* pure luck that she'd seen them first at all. She hadn't been looking for them. She saw them while staring out the window, ignoring the math lesson, and thinking of Charlie Evans. Her eyes focused on the vehicles, like tiny ants in the distance, jetting down the highway and then, as they crept closer, they morphed into something delicious and exciting. She had been wishing so hard for summer to start, and then, there they were, rumbling down Route 9.

Other people likely saw them, too, but Tessa was the first one who said out loud that they were there.

That night, Tessa watched as Lulu pushed her food around on her plate. Tessa knew this meant that either Lulu was being dramatic or that she didn't like the quail her father was trying out on them that evening.

"What rides are you going on?" Lulu asked.

"Every one," Tessa said, "and all the scary ones, for sure."

Tessa was betting on dramatic, because Lulu always liked her father's cooking. He and Lulu had the same taste for the untried.

"It will be better this year than last," Lulu said.

"Of course it will be," Tessa said.

On that they could agree.

Tessa watched Lulu eat three bites quietly and then listened as Lulu asked the question she already knew the answer to.

"Who are you going with?"

"Celina, of course."

Celina was Tessa's best friend. They had been planning their first unchaperoned trip to the carnival all year long.

"Can I come, too?" Lulu asked.

"No," Tessa said. "Definitely not." This could spoil everything.

Just the thought of Lulu going with them made Tessa's curls tighten.

"I won't be any trouble," Lulu said.

"Be nice to your sister," their mother said, and gave the girls a look. Sometimes their mother could look as tough as her tattoos. She knew how to settle things with her eyes. Tessa had tried to learn that trick, but things didn't always go the way she wanted when she did it.

Tessa had to admit that, in truth, Lulu was not that troublesome. She had tagged along with Tessa and Celina for so many years that in a way she was an unofficial third to their best friendship. Tessa knew the rules of being the older sister meant that Lulu would either come with them or they'd be condemned to going to the carnival with parents. Despite Tessa's annoyance that Lulu would slow down their fun, she couldn't deny her sister the freedom to roam with her and Celina on the fairgrounds without the burden of parents. But that didn't stop Tessa from doing everything she could to make it clear that it was still unfair.

"I'm not my sister's keeper," Tessa said to her mother, and then slammed her fist on the table so that her dinner plate jumped.

Her fury was useless. Lulu would tag along.

Tessa told Celina at lunch as they watched Charlie Evans throw a ball around with Dylan and Tony and wondered what kinds of plans they were making.

"Lulu wants to tag along with us," Tessa said.

Celina's face dropped.

"But she's in eighth grade," Celina said. "We're practically sopho-mores."

"I know, I know," Tessa said.

"Not cool, Tessa," Celina said.

"She'll behave," Tessa said. "I made her swear."

They both knew that Tessa didn't have any choice. But Tessa couldn't help blaming Lulu just a little.

Their father dropped them off at the mouth of the carnival, and he gave them each forty dollars for tickets and rides and hot dogs and games and told them to *be careful* and to *have fun*.

He barely got the words out before the girls shrugged him off and ran straight into the night, disappearing into the noise and the lights.

There was so much to see, and although the girls had been to the carnival every year since they were little, this time everything about it seemed new.

"You'd better act cool," Tessa said.

"OK," Lulu said.

"You'd better stay quiet," Tessa said.

"OK," Lulu said.

"You'd better do what I say," Tessa said.

"You got it," Lulu said. And then she smiled big—the smile of a girl who could taste her first bite of freedom.

"What should we do first?" Tessa asked once they had met up with Celina at the assigned spot.

"It's like we're grown-ups," Celina whispered. And the three girls nodded in unison, then took a moment to savor being old enough to go on their own to a place that had always seemed doomed to being the territory of family outings.

"Look." Tessa grabbed Celina's arm.

She pointed to a ticket booth. There stood Charlie Evans with Dylan, Tony, and Lionel. Tessa stilled herself and held her breath; Charlie's looks had that effect on her.

"We should hook up with them," Celina said. She knew how to seize the moment. Tessa loved that about her best friend.

"That's Charlie Evans," Lulu said. She had heard all about him and his dreamy looks from Tessa, but this was the first time she'd seen him off the football field without all that protective gear.

"Yeah, what do you think?" Tessa asked.

Lulu shrugged. She seemed unimpressed.

"Charlie will know how to have fun," Celina said. "If you know what I mean."

"What do you mean?" Lulu asked.

"I thought you didn't like him like that," Tessa said.

"I don't like him like that," Celina said.

"What do you mean?" Lulu asked again.

Tessa liked him like that. She admired him from afar, touched his locker when she walked by, and said hello to him every morning as they passed each other in the hallway. She even laughed at the jokes he made at the table next to theirs at lunchtime. Celina was the one who didn't like Charlie. She didn't like his dumb hair, his cleft chin, his anything.

"What do you mean?" Lulu asked a third time.

Tessa and Celina gave each other looks.

"Boys!" Tessa said.

"A boy is a boy is a boy. And Charlie's got enough boys with him to go around. We should all go get one," Celina said.

"Boys," Lulu said. She said it quietly, like she was saying something forbidden. Then she giggled, covering her mouth with her tiny white hand. Sometimes she acted younger than 13. Tessa felt embarrassed for Lulu. Tessa saw Celina roll her eyes. Tessa rolled her eyes back at Celina in agreement. And just like that, they were in sync again.

It was then that Tessa noticed that Lulu was wearing Tessa's favorite pair of skinny jeans. Lulu had not asked permission to go into her room and borrow them. Tessa was peeved that they looked better on Lulu. She should probably just let her sister have them but she knew that she wouldn't. Whenever she went trolling through her sister's drawers, she never found anything good to steal—just bangle brace-lets, colorful scarves that no one knew how to wear, and unused vin-tage buttons from their grandma's collection.

Sometimes Tessa wished that she was the prettier sister. When Tessa looked at Lulu, she wondered why it was that Lulu got the better nose. The nicer legs. The shinier, straighter hair. Tessa worried some-times that people felt sorry for her because she was not round-faced, but made of angles. She dreaded that the truth might be that the ar-rangement of DNA hadn't worked quite right on her parents' first try for a baby, and she imagined that the combination of sperm and egg had worked better the second time around. Or worse, that maybe her parents had loved each other more when they had made Lulu.

Tessa shook the thought off like a bug. As she twitched the notion away, Celina and Lulu looked at her quizzically, imagined that they saw the bug, too, and helped her to shoo it away.

Tessa tried to smooth her hair, but the curls sprang back.

"Charlie!" Celina said. "Charlie!"

Charlie and his friends looked up at the exact same moment and all smiled their young man smiles, the ones that made the three girls fluttery. The girls collapsed toward each other, linking hands made uncomfortable with the wearing of new chunky rings purchased just for tonight.

Charlie waved them over and the girls moved toward him and his friends, clutching each other as though they had scored a victory. And in a way they had. They had won attention. And for the moment that was just as good as any of Celina's swim-meet medals or Tessa's certificates of merit in science. Maybe even *better*. They sashayed over to the boys, swinging their hips in a way that they had never done before.

When they got to the ticket booth, Jasper Kleine bumped into Tessa hard. He wasn't with Charlie and his boys. In fact, he wasn't with anyone because he was a loner. If he did hang out, he hung out with other lost boys. The ones who cut class and got high. The ones who rode their speedboats too fast on the river. The ones who had guitars and mountain bikes. The ones who wore pieces of leather tied around their wrists as if they had made a secret promise to themselves. These boys were the ones that everyone steered clear of because secretly everyone worried that strangeness was catching.

Jasper had bumped into Tessa because he wasn't looking where he was going. He didn't stop. He didn't apologize. He just kept walking. He was too busy counting his tickets. It seemed like he had enough tickets to do every single thing at the carnival—*twice.*

To Tessa he smelled like a mixture of a latte, pot, pond scum, and sweat. But it was pleasant, the way that a skunk was pleasant, or garlic, or patchouli, even though her mother said that patchouli smelled like feet. Tessa liked the smell of feet. Tessa's eyes followed him as he walked down the midway. He was so sure of himself. She noticed how happy he was to be on the outside of everything. She was a little jealous that he was glad to be alone.

Tessa wondered what Jasper would do first. Would he go on a ride? Would he enter one of the tents? Would he play a game and try to win a prize? If he did win, who would he give the prize to? Tessa had never seen him with anyone specifically.

Tessa always had someone to hang around with, like her sister or Celina. She never would go anywhere alone. She always ran in a pack. Everyone did that. But not Jasper. She wondered what that would be like, to go somewhere alone. But then she stopped wondering because Charlie was standing in front of her, looking at her from under his impossibly long brown eyelashes. And then Tessa was too busy blushing, and trying to look as pretty as she could despite her imagined genetic deficiencies. She couldn't spare the energy to think about Jasper anymore.

"Let's go," Charlie said.

The whole group of them lurched into motion.

The promise of the carnival washed away all of Tessa's musings about Jasper. Her insecurities faded, and she was overwhelmed by the big and the bright and the fantastic possibilities of the night that stretched in front of them. In that light surely she was pretty. Everyone was.

Tessa thought they were a happy bunch. They looked like they all belonged together. She felt they'd all be best friends forever. Tessa tried to ignore the booths that looked like teeth, and made the carnival feel like a mouth. She concentrated on the other things the fair had to offer: the games with stuffed animals and t-shirts as prizes, the Ferris wheel, the teacup ride, the fun house, the haunted house and the curiosity sideshow tent.

They started with the games. Gathering and jostling each other by the beanbag throw. When no one won anything, they blamed their loss on the games being rigged, which they most likely were.

"This blows, we'll never win."

"It's not fair."

"Life's not fair."

"Well what should we do?"

"We should ride every single ride till we get sick."

"They look so rickety."

"I don't do rides."

"Statistics say that the rides are safe."

"If you say so."

"How about the curiosity sideshow tent?" Tessa said.

Everyone stopped talking, and Tessa felt as though she had a stain on her shirt. Or something was stuck in her teeth. Or she had blood on her pants. Whatever it was, one thing was for sure—she had said something wrong.

"I don't want to go in there, it's just going to be things in formaldehyde," Celina said, putting a hand on her hip. Sometimes Celina could be stubborn because she always wanted to be the girl with the plan.

Everyone looked at Celina waiting for her to come up with an alternative. Tessa looked toward the curiosity sideshow tent. Lulu looked, too.

"But it will be dark," Lulu said.

"What?" Celina's eyes widened.

Lulu looked at the boys.

"Dark," Tessa repeated what her sister had said.

Tessa loved her sister something fierce at that moment. Maybe it was worth having her around because she was handy as backup.

"Oooh," everyone said.

They were all on the same side again. Darkness meant the possibility of hand holding or kissing. Darkness was good when it was mixed with boys.

"Good idea," Charlie said, staring right down into Tessa—right down to the parts of her that were secret.

Tessa and her heart sighed. She would do anything to be alone inside a dark tent with Charlie. She could just picture how the whole thing was going to go down. It would be perfect. She would pretend to be scared and maybe grab his hand for support. She would clutch him tightly and not let go. And he would keep holding her hand because everyone knew that holding hands felt so good.

The sign on the tent said ODD CURIOSITIES INSIDE!!! It also

said that people should proceed into the tent in twos. As her group stood in line, patiently waiting for their turn, Tessa tried to calculate her odds of going in with Charlie. It was like a math word problem from school: If two people in a jostling line wanted to be paired off together, and there were an odd number of kids, what are the odds that person x and person y will go into the tent together?

She had never been good at math, always staring out the window instead. So she hung back a little bit so that she would be next to him.

If they were in the tent together, then he would notice her and her alone, and they would emerge from the exhibit as a *couple*.

She just had to go in with him. This was her chance.

Tessa tried to look as though she was thinking of other things. She tried to look casual. She laughed a little too loudly when Charlie spoke about his riverboat. She studied the dirt mixed with sawdust and how it kicked up on her shoe and stuck there. All the while she made sure she always kept herself next to Charlie. Lulu stood next to her sister as though she wanted to go into the tent with Tessa. It was as if she was too scared to go in with a boy by herself.

Lulu is such a baby, Tessa thought. Tessa was glad that she was 15. Glad that their parents called her a *young lady* and not a *girl*. Glad that she didn't still have her dollhouse in her bedroom. She knew that Lulu still sometimes rearranged the furniture in hers and pretended she was dusting. The truth was that Lulu was still more girl than young lady.

Celina went first with Tony. Dylan went in with a girl they knew from school whom he'd grabbed into the line. Tessa hung back, and so Lulu hung back, and so Charlie hung back, and pretty soon the three of them were at the front of the line.

"Next," said the girl in the carnival costume of red pinstripes and black vest.

Tessa stepped forward only to find the girl's striped arm blocking her way.

"Only two at a time," the girl said, snapping her gum.

And suddenly, Tessa was outside, looking at the closing flap, and her Charlie was heading into the curiosity sideshow tent with Lulu.

"Next," the girl said and opened the tent flap again. Tessa didn't want to go into the freak tent anymore. She began to step aside to let the people behind her go, but then a hand appeared gently on her shoulder and guided her toward the total blackness. There was nothing to do but go in.

"Freaky," the voice belonging to the arm said.

Tessa turned around and stood face-to-face with Jasper Kleine. She thought she could see that Jasper was smiling. Her eyes adjusted to the dimness in time to see her sister and Charlie disappear into the next section of the tent. She didn't want to stop and see the thing in the jar sitting illuminated on the table that Jasper was steering her toward. She wanted to follow Charlie and Lulu into the next room and say something clever. But suddenly a fear choked her and that fear made her feet unwilling to step forward and pursue them.

She didn't want to look at Jasper.

So she looked at the jar.

Inside was a twisted creature that looked like a shaved rat with wings. It was pink and veiny. The wings had wet feathers that limply clung together, but they didn't look natural. They looked pressed on.

"You can tell they just stitched together two animals," Jasper said. He was moving toward the next room. "Rat and bat. Come on."

Jasper held open the curtain for her. She stepped through. They moved from room to room as though in a dream. The curiosities were laughable. It was the darkness that was frightening. And the music;

it was like a timpani or like wind pushed through drowning lungs. It was a ghostly soundtrack.

Jasper kept talking, commenting on the various beasts on display. Tessa said nothing. She strained her ears through the silent moments in an attempt to hear what Charlie and Lulu were laughing about up ahead. But she never caught anything. She would have to hear all about it later.

"Where are we going next?" Jasper asked when they reached the last room.

He was so close to her. She could feel his breath on her face, and she could smell him. If she moved the tiniest bit, her lips would be on his.

She felt strange. Strangled. Joyous. Angry. Tingly.

"We're not," she said.

She said it to hurt him.

His eyes went from soft to wounded. Then Tessa felt bad, but didn't say so. She just looked at him harder, wishing that he would get the hint and go away.

"OK, I don't like groups anyway," he said, and he stepped out of the tent and went on his way, leaving her alone.

She was sure that her disappointment had made her hair curl more. There was only one way to face Lulu and Charlie—with smooth hair. It was easier to look like she didn't care if her hair was straighter. She didn't want her wild corkscrew curls to betray her hurt.

She tried to coax it down with a little spit, hoping to tame it before she emerged. She ran her hand through her hair. No good. It was still a mass of tangles.

chapter
two

time to get up.

sssssteady.

NOTHING CHANGED IN THE NIGHT

NO MATTER HOW MUCH I HOPED IT MIGHT.

SOMETIMES I WISH THAT WHILE I'M SLEEPING,

SOME KIND OF MAGIC WILL STEAL THROUGH MY DREAMS AND MAKE ME NORMAL AGAIN.

I'M A FOOL.

MOM.

DAD.

WHO AM I KIDDING?

THEY'RE EXACTLY WHERE THEY WERE YESTERDAY.

AND THE DAY BEFORE THAT.

AND THE WEEK BEFORE **THAT**.

jusssst go QUICKLY.

I'M GOING NOW.

I'M LEAVING.

I'M GONE.

chapter three

The first thing Tessa noticed when she emerged from the curiosity sideshow tent was Lulu and Charlie's fingers curled around each other's. Their eyes were shiny and even if they didn't know it for sure yet themselves, it was clear to her that Charlie and Lulu were now boyfriend and girlfriend.

A black hole emerged inside of Tessa, making everything good about the evening fall inward until it disappeared.

But Lulu had a warm smile. She gave Tessa and Celina a look, and the girls excused themselves from the group of boys to go to the bathroom so that they could talk. They grabbed each other, and held hands and skipped on the way there.

Tessa couldn't help but squeeze Lulu a little too forcefully and laugh in an unnatural way that hurt even her own ears.

Lulu laughed back. But it was so pure that it drowned out any unsavoriness among them.

"Well?" Celina said, breathlessly.

"Well . . ." Lulu said, turning red.

"Well," Tessa said, trying not to sound bitter; trying to hold her face in an expression that resembled happiness for her sister's new status.

"He kissed me. Right by the jackalope. He kissed me!" Lulu said. She touched her heart as she said it. Her face flushed. Her voice cracked.

It was her first kiss. Lulu was a late bloomer compared with her sister. Tessa knew that much. Lulu was always much more interested in books. She had a romantic idea about what a first kiss, a first beau, a first anything should be. She was such a girl that way. Tessa had made out with her first boy back in sixth grade. It was nothing special, just a boy named Keith in the corner of a dark room. He kissed her with an open mouth, blowing his cheeks out like a puffer fish. She did not particularly enjoy it, but she had done it. She'd kissed other boys at make out parties, in closets, or when the bottle pointed at her. But she'd never kissed Charlie.

Lulu sighed. It was a real sigh. The kind that makes everyone around feel giddy about life. Even Tessa's mood brightened for a moment.

How could she not love a sister who believed in that kind of magic? Deep down Tessa knew that it was a piece of magic that they shared. Tessa, too, felt that kisses could be more than a grope in the dark or too much wetness; and if she were honest, truly honest, she would wish for Lulu only kisses that curled toes. Only magical kisses with boys like Charlie—just as she was sure that Lulu would wish that for her.

But magic like that can grow twisted and dark if it doesn't come to the light. Tessa had so many kisses that meant nothing, it made her think that maybe magic didn't exist. Meanwhile, Lulu had one kiss that bubbled all the light up to the surface.

"Was it good?" Celina asked. "Did you like it?"

Lulu nodded emphatically. Yes. Yes. Yes. It was good. Celina grabbed Lulu's hand and turned her back on Tessa.

"I made out with Tony," Celina said. "But it was nothing. It was just something to do."

Celina was like that. She liked to make out with boys by the dozen and it meant nothing. She didn't believe that the quality of kisses mattered, just the number of them. She was leaning over the sink, dangerously close to a puddle of water, unsmudging her blue eyeliner.

Tessa felt that quality might be more meaningful than quantity, but quantity might get a girl a reputation. Tessa and Celina had long ago decided that it was unclear whether a reputation was a good or a bad thing to have. They thought that perhaps even a bad reputation might be a good thing to have.

A reputation got you noticed.

Charlie had a reputation for being a good boy.

Jasper had a reputation for being a weirdo.

And everyone knew who they were.

For a long time no one noticed Tessa and Celina. And they had wanted that to change.

Celina and Lulu each had a reputation now.

Tessa felt the change in the air. Saw it in all of their bodies. Tessa watched as Celina and Lulu stepped closer to each other, as though kissing in the curiosity sideshow tent with a boy had somehow united them.

"How about you, Tessa?" Celina asked. "Did you make out?"

"No," Tessa said. "I was alone."

"You didn't go in with anyone?" Celina asked.

"No." Tessa examined the pattern on the sink counter.

It was easier to lie, otherwise it was complicated.

If she said that she had been in the tent with Jasper, there would be questions. And she wasn't sure that she could explain that Jasper had whispered witty things about each weird object they saw in the tent and that she had bitten the insides of her cheeks so he wouldn't know that she had wanted to laugh. That she almost didn't mind when he caught her by the elbow when she tripped on an extension cord. That being with him in that tent had a different feeling than what she felt when she hung out with her friends. If Tessa said those things out loud, they might not be understood.

Besides, there was a bigger truth. She wasn't in there with Charlie, and he was the only person she had wanted to be with. So in truth, no one else counted. Her mood, almost changed, reverted back to bittersweet.

Tessa wondered what kind of sister she would be if she weren't truly happy for Lulu. Would she be a mean sister, like those in fairy-tale books they both loved? When she spoke would only toads and bugs fly out of her mouth? Would she be condemned to be the true ugly one? Would her road always be dark and barren? Would her soul grow more and more twisted?

Lulu sighed again and then reached into her purse for some lip gloss. She made a big show of applying it, as though the kissing had made it necessary for her to be extra glossy.

Inside herself, Tessa reached for the light left behind by the sigh. But it slipped away into the growing, gnawing hole inside of her. But then a moment later, Lulu shifted, and the twosome became a threesome again. Tessa didn't have to worry. They would never leave her out.

"Oh," Lulu said. "You should have come with us."

Lulu said it sincerely. As if she wouldn't have minded trading in the kisses with Charlie for Tessa not having to be alone in the curiosity sideshow tent. She stuck her hand out and squeezed her sister's hand sympathetically.

"But then you wouldn't have been alone with Charlie," Tessa said. "And then you wouldn't have made out. And then you wouldn't have a summer boyfriend."

"Let's not keep your boyfriend waiting!" Celina said.

"Right," Lulu said. And then blushed again. And then sighed. And then gazed dreamily at the door. Until they all ran out the door and headed back to the boys.

Despite her resolve to be happy for her sister, Tessa couldn't help but think that it was supposed to be her sharing Charlie's Slurpee, her holding his hand, her wearing his varsity jacket when the night got chillier. Tessa watched Charlie and Lulu whispering to each other and stealing kisses while in line for all the rides.

After all, hadn't Charlie talked to *her* at school? Hadn't he stolen glances at *her* during lunch? Didn't he sometimes say nice things to *her*, like, "I like your sweater," or "Nice answer in Ms. Durbin's class," or "Hey, do you want potato chips?" And didn't those things mean something? Tessa could string a thousand tiny moments together and weave a story in which Charlie liked *her*.

But she could not deny the way that Charlie leaned in toward Lulu. Shared his cotton candy with her. Held her purse for her. Pushed the long hair off of her face.

Celina spent the night bouncing from Dylan to Tony, and they were all happy about it. Tessa watched as each of them tried to one-up the other in order to win Celina's undivided attention. Celina didn't want lose any morsel of it and she strung them along, convincing each that they would be hers exclusively.

Lionel was too smart to get caught up in that game, so he had turned to Tessa. Lionel did all the nice things that a good boy would do, he bought her tickets to all the rides, he held her bag when she took her turn at playing the water pistol game, he won her a plush space monkey, but to no avail. Tessa ignored Lionel's attempts at sweetness, and he eventually gave up and trailed along behind the group, occupying himself with something on his phone.

And then just when she thought she couldn't stand the night for one more moment, the chance to leave presented itself. Tessa grabbed on to it.

It was when they were on the Tilt-A-Whirl. Or, as Celina called it, the "Tilt-A-Hurl." Tessa had eaten a polish sausage with curly fries and a soda pop. She had a strong stomach, but the bubbles of the soda made her want to burp. She tried holding it in, but as the ride slung around, the bubbles in her chest grew larger. She knew that she could keep it down. But when she stepped off the ride, she let out a big belch that lifted the food up her esophagus.

"Are you OK?" Celina asked. The burp had been loud and gurgly. She knew this was her chance.

"No," Tessa said. She forced another burp and this time did not hold back and threw up in a garbage can.

"Oh, no!" Lulu said, leaving Charlie's side, which is what Tessa had to admit she'd wanted the whole night. Lulu came to her and whispered soothing words and rubbed her back. Even Charlie went to get her a glass of water and paid attention to her. Tessa cried a little, and everyone thought that it was because of the throwing up and the not feeling well, but really it was because Lulu had gotten

Charlie and Tessa was upset about it no matter how much she truly loved her sister. She was jealous. But no one needed to know that.

The only thing everyone needed to know was that Tessa wanted to go home.

"I'll come with you," Lulu said.

"No, Lulu," Charlie said. "Stay."

That wounded Tessa, and she flinched as though the words had scratched her insides.

Lulu didn't even hesitate.

"No," she said. "I have to take care of my sister."

They left together, Lulu with her arm around her sister, holding her up, Tessa feeling a little bit victorious. Tessa faked being ill all weekend and Lulu stayed with her, playing card games and drinking ginger ale and eating dry crackers with her in solidarity, even though she wasn't sick herself. Even though everyone else was spending all their free time together at the carnival. Even though Charlie called or texted every hour and the carnival would be leaving soon.

Tessa couldn't understand because given the choice between boy-attention and no boy-attention she would have chosen boy-attention, especially if the boy in question was Charlie Evans and *especially* if it meant he could be her boyfriend. Tessa was quietly impressed with Lulu's confidence in how she handled the attention. She wondered where she could have gotten it from. Is that what being pretty did to someone? Did it give you an impossible amount of patience? Was it another thing that Lulu inherited that Tessa hadn't?

She started to study Lulu's laissez-faire attitude. Perhaps she could learn something from Lulu, instead of succumbing to the passions that always burst out of her. The ones that made her turn the lights low and listen to moody music and made her scream at her parents for being so clueless when in fact she had never even given them a clue to begin with. The passions that got her in trouble up front and hurt her more in the long run. The ones that made her hair curl up even tighter.

Tessa was glad to have her sister all to herself. But it troubled her that Lulu was ignoring Charlie. Tessa's heart went out to Charlie. What must he be thinking? Could his feelings be hurt? Each text sounded a little bit more desperate. It was Saturday night and Lulu chose to climb into bed with Tessa. They watched movies, whispered about their stupid parents, and made plans for summer. And for a moment Tessa couldn't tell if they were thirteen and fifteen years old or seven and nine.

"I'm going to put straightener in my hair," Tessa said.

"Me, too."

"I'm going to learn how to ride a horse."

"Me, too."

"I'm going invent a new kind of cookie."

"Me, too."

"You can't just do everything that I do," Tessa said.

But it had always been like that, Lulu always copying her, always acting like a second shadow. Lulu always looking to Tessa to lead the way.

Lulu lay her head on the pillow, her features flattened by the light of the flat-screen T.V. The cell phone buzzed, a new text from Charlie had arrived. Lulu showed it to Tessa. Tessa felt a stab but didn't say anything. Lulu put the phone back down.

"Aren't you going to write him back?" Tessa asked

"Should I?" Lulu asked.

Tessa shrugged. She didn't know. She couldn't lead the way this time. Being older had taught her nothing about boys except that they were infinitely mysterious. All she knew was that she would have written him back, or gone to the carnival, or made a firm date right away to be alone and kiss more. She wouldn't have hung out with her sister all weekend. But she didn't want to encourage Lulu toward Charlie.

Celina came over to check on her friend and to try to change Lulu's mind about going to the carnival Sunday before it closed. Celina didn't want to go alone, and while there were other girls to hang out with, Tessa was her best friend. And Lulu was her best friend's sister, so was a much better substitute than other girls she might have gone with. Besides, Lulu was Celina's best chance at hanging out with Charlie and the boys. And Celina was interested in hanging out with boys.

"It's so boring without you, Tessa. Don't you feel better?" Celina asked.

"No."

"Well, can't you lend me Lulu?"

"No."

"But Lulu, aren't you worried that Charlie will kiss another girl?" Celina asked.

Tessa looked at Lulu. Lulu's hands were twisting in the same way that she used to do when she heard a ghost story or stayed up late watching a scary movie.

"Then I guess he doesn't like me very much if he can't wait until the next time he sees me to kiss me again," Lulu said.

"That is so mature," Celina said. "You're going to do OK in high school next year."

Then Lulu excused herself and went to her room. And that was that. When Tessa passed by the open door, she saw Lulu kneeling on the floor in front of her dollhouse. She was surrounded by paper towels. The sun was coming in through the window, making everything look golden. Lulu looked enormous, sitting there among the tiny chairs, tables, and beds. Tessa watched as Lulu cleaned off each item and placed it delicately back in the house. The furniture was now re-arranged. And as Lulu placed each doll into its room, she whispered secrets into their tiny ears.

Tessa felt sorry for her sister. She couldn't be sure, but a thought struck Tessa. Maybe Lulu wasn't trying to be cool or grown up about the whole thing at all. Maybe Lulu had been *scared*.

chapter four

IF I LOOK TOO DEEPLY AT HIM,

WILL HE TURN TO STONE?

too sslow.

you've ssseen him, it's done.

it's OVER.

he's. fine.

he's fine.

he'sss fine.

RRRIIINNNNGGG

chapter five

The river cut through town neatly, running east to west, flowing out to sea. Most houses sat on the hills overlooking the water, but some had backyards that stretched down to touch the riverbanks.

In the winters, the river whitened with snow and ice. In the spring, it broke and ran and rushed quickly by. In the summer, it slowed and rambled, and in the fall it clogged with leaves.

No matter where you lived, everyone in town had a boat docked somewhere on the river.

Celina's backyard sloped gently toward a stretch of the river shaded by trees. When they were little, Tessa and Lulu believed fairies lived in all the woods around the county where they lived. Local legend told of a man who got lost in the woods, took a nap, and wandered out one hundred years later. Tessa and Lulu would take naps by the trees hoping that they would wake up older and in the future. They never did.

School had been out for a week, and the carnival been gone for two, leaving a muddy mess of papers, garbage, and sawdust in its wake.

Few would look at the field where it had stood and believe that any kind of magic occurred there. But that field had been full of kisses. And rides. And blushes. There had been hearts that caught in throats, eyes that glanced discreetly, and hands that reached for parts forbidden.

Tessa hadn't experienced any of those things, and so when she passed the field on the way to Celina's house on her bicycle, she only saw the garbage that was left behind. The empty filthy field matched exactly the wreckage of her feelings for Charlie. Charlie who had taken Lulu out exactly three times so far. Lulu came back from each of those dates blooming.

It was the first barbecue of the summer; the one that celebrated Independence Day. At Celina's insistence, Tessa had reluctantly started to bring Lulu around more, and the girls, now a firm threesome, had conspired together to invite the boys to the Fourth of July celebration. There was going to be a big fireworks display set off by the firemen from a barge on the river. The whole valley would be able to watch from anywhere in the three towns. Celina's parents had even invited the mayor to watch from their lawn.

The party started early, and while Celina's parents made mixed drinks and had adult conversations on the patio, the girls were nervous because Charlie, Lionel, Tony, and Dylan were late.

"Do you think they'll come?" Celina asked. "Did Charlie say they would?"

Lulu nodded. She was now the one among them who had the inside information. She showed her authority by texting Charlie and then showing his response, which he'd signed with x's and o's.

Celina clapped in approval.

"Lulu, go help Celina's mom," Tessa said.

"She already said she didn't need any help," Lulu said.

No matter how hard Tessa tried to shoo Lulu elsewhere and get Celina alone, Lulu remained. She was always there, never getting the hint, acting like a shiny new thing.

Eventually, the boys showed up with brushed hair, dress shirts, and bags of candy.

The adults remembered what it was like to be young, and so they watched the teens closely for the first hour, making sure that no beer was stolen and that all the boys and girls hands were in proper places at all times. But as the day dragged on, and the liquor poured more freely, the adults became more concerned with their own drama and loud laughter. By the time the sun set, they had full confidence that no girls would get knocked up and no lines would get crossed.

Tessa, Celina, Lulu, and the boys disappeared through the trees to spread blankets on the patch of grass near the dock to get a better view of the sky. As the sun sank behind the hills, making the river go from silvery to muted brown, they chattered nervously. Charlie sat next to Lulu, holding her hand and whispering quietly. It must have been something funny because Lulu laughed quietly, and no matter how far Tessa stretched she couldn't catch what he was saying. Lionel, Tony, and Dylan flanked Celina, telling gross stories about zits and poop and other bodily things. Celina pretended to be disgusted but actually was loving every minute of it. Tessa busied herself putting the plates out. Tony broke off from the others and awkwardly tried to help her dole out the food they'd brought down from the patio. The light faded, the shadows lengthened, the sun disappeared, and when it was dark enough, the first evening stars came out.

They all listened to the sound of rushing water and shouts on the barges as the firemen prepared to start the show. They lay down on the blankets and Tessa watched as Charlie turned toward Lulu and kissed her. Celina turned to Dylan, who was the boy that she had chosen for the night, most likely because he was the closest.

"You're cute," Tessa heard her say, and she watched as Celina pulled him to her and began to kiss him.

Their lips smacked together so loudly that Tessa, not even a foot away, thought that it sounded like a cow chewing. Lionel cursed, having lost out on his chance with Celina. He threw a clump of dirt at the boat that bobbed on the water in front of them.

Tony screwed up his courage and dove in for Tessa's lips. But he missed as Tessa moved away.

No, thought Tessa as she dodged him. *This is not the kiss I want.*

She had kissed Tony before and had felt his papery lips and probing tongue. But there was no spark. And she could see the sparks flying all around her. They flew around Lulu and Charlie like a swarm, and even Celina and Dylan had some. If Tessa was going to kiss, she wanted some sparks.

The leaves on the trees rustled, their long branches sleepily waving her toward them as though they were promising something different than what was being offered on the checkered blankets.

"I have to go to the bathroom," Tessa said.

"But the show is about to start," Tony said, his voice low, as though that would somehow change her mind and tempt her to his lips.

A flare shot into the night. The air filled with a dramatic string overture, the music skipping across the valley as the first starburst hit the air.

"I'll go in the woods," Tessa said. "I'll be right back."

She left him looking satisfied that she'd come back with an empty bladder and a soul full of passion for him. He lay back on his arms, smug with that thought.

Tessa stumbled toward the trees. She tried not to look at the tangled legs and arms of the others as the colors in the sky lit them up softly. Fireworks sprayed the sky and exploded in time to the music. Tessa could relate to the display—very dramatic, and the music—all brass. The light fell from the sky toward the river. Tessa felt as though she were bursting inside in a hot and violent way. She felt like a bomb and not a pretty blast of light.

As she entered the woods, she tripped on a root and found herself on the ground with the leaves and the dirt. Her eyes stung with earth and she heard a twig crack.

She was not alone.

"Who's there?" she asked the trees.

She wanted this night to be over. She imagined falling asleep. She wondered if she did if time would pass, like the man in the legend, and she'd wake up and run out of the woods one hundred years later. She would like that. The darkness was peppered every few seconds or so by reds, whites, and blues, and so she knew that she was still awake.

She saw a body emerge from behind a tree. Was it a deer? A bear? A bird? No. It was a boy. He slid quietly toward her, his step sure, as though he belonged in those woods and knew them well even in the dark.

"It's me," a voice said.

Jasper.

The dark was lightened suddenly by a series of white bursts that lit up the sky like it was high noon. She could see him perfectly. Every line of him. Every thread. Every bone.

"You have dirt on your face," he said.

He came over to her and sat down. He took the bottom of his t-shirt and lifted it up to her eyes and began wiping her cheeks clean.

"Were you spying on us?" Tessa asked.

"No," he said. "I live next door."

Tessa had never known where Jasper lived. She knew nothing at all about him, except that he was strange. That he wore t-shirts with images and phrases that she didn't understand. And that all those things combined made him seem so sure of himself in a way that no one else she knew was.

"This is the best spot to watch from. And I heard voices. I wanted to see who was here," he said. "It was all of you."

Tessa closed her eyes but could still see the lights from behind her lids. She felt the explosions in her chest. She sympathized with the sudden blast of trumpets.

She wondered why he didn't just join them when he saw them all sitting on the blankets. He would have been welcome to the fried chicken and to the hot dogs. He could have enjoyed the potato salad. He could have shared the last piece of chocolate cake.

"We have some blankets," she said. "We have food and a good view."

"I hate Lionel," he said.

"He's not so bad," Tessa said.

"Lionel made me eat paste," he said.

"That doesn't sound like Lionel," Tessa said.

"Well, people aren't always what they seem," he said.

"I ate paste once, just to try it," Tessa said.

"I didn't want to try it," Jasper said.

"That was a long time ago though, right?" Tessa asked.

"I guess," Jasper said. "Everybody dared him to do it. And he did. I don't understand why people do what other people tell them to do."

Tessa knew that truthfully, Jasper would not have been welcomed on the blankets the way that he had welcomed her into the woods. They would make fun of his hair. Or his sweater. Or his sunken chest. They would all laugh under their breath and Jasper wouldn't get that he was the joke.

She heard a sound. Her name. They were probably calling her. Wondering where she was. But none of them would likely leave the blankets and come fetch her from the woods.

She felt Jasper take her hand, and she did not let it go. His hand felt moist, but curiously familiar, as though it were a part of her. As though it were her very own hand. She leaned her head against the bark of the tree and the roughness of it made her open her eyes. Jasper was looking at her, and bursts of falling lights dazzled, making his hair glow like fire.

There were things deep inside her bubbling up that she could not explain. There was his hand holding hers tightly. There was sweat on the soft fuzz of his boyish mustache.

She moved toward him and put her lips on his.

These were actions that she knew once done, could not be taken back.

chapter six

FIRST PERIOD

THEY'RE ALL AFRAID OF ME.

GIVE ME SOMEWHERE TO STAND AND I WILL MOVE THE EARTH
—ARCHIMEDES

MY NAME IS NOBODY
—HOMER

THEY'RE WONDERING, "HOW LONG DOES IT TAKE BEFORE LOOKING AT ME MAKES THEIR FLESH HARDEN?"

THEIR SKIN CRACK AND TURN GRAY?

remember

first derivative

$f'(x) = \lim_{h \to 0} \frac{f(x+h) - f(x)}{h}$

OR THEIR BONES BECOME HEAVY?

WHEN DO THEY TURN TO STONE?

YES?

I HAVE TO GO TO THE BATHROOM.

KLIK

I WANT TO GO BACK TO THE WAY THINGS WERE.

unlikely.

impossible.

there he goes!

FOLLOW HIM.

GO.

DON'T LOSE HIM!

chapter seven

Tessa wondered if that one night of kissing Jasper had made her look different because after two weeks of kissing Charlie, everyone agreed on one thing: Lulu looked different.

Lulu looked light on her feet and translucent, as though she were made of Bohemian glass and caught the light in a special way. And when she walked, she *glided*. Or, she was always dancing. She had a secret skip that couldn't be ignored by anyone. Lulu glowed with all the kissing that she had done with Charlie. And Lulu kissed Charlie whenever she could. Lulu kissed him on the porch. On the dock. In the diner. At the movies. In his barn. In his beat up old car. She kissed him in public for everyone to see. They kissed in a way that made sure everyone around them knew how they felt.

At the breakfast table, their parents would tease Lulu until she turned red, and when her protests didn't make them stop, she would resign herself to shoveling spoonful after spoonful of cereal into her mouth.

"You are in love, Lulu," their father would say.

"Your very first love." Their mother would sigh.

Then Tessa watched as their parents would laugh and play with each others' fingers as they looked at each other tenderly. As though the magic of Lulu's first love had been catching and had rekindled something inside of them that they had misplaced for a while. Her father's piercings would sparkle. Her mother's tattoos would ripple with color and almost come to life.

Tessa knew that she could have said something about her own kiss. Sometimes at night, in bed, she would kiss the tips of her own fingers and remember Jasper's lips. Sometimes she wondered about her one kiss with him; wondered whether he would agree that it was the only kiss that had ever seemed to matter.

That year, no one was going to summer camp because of the economy. Almost all of the kids would be staying in town, forced to entertain themselves. Celina invited the sisters over every day. After breakfast, Tessa and Lulu hopped on their bikes and wound their way over. Tessa wished that sometimes Celina would not remember to invite Lulu. But since that didn't work, Tessa would remind Lulu that she could always hang out with her own friends.

"But they don't understand about boys like Celina and you do," Lulu said.

And that would always win Tessa over.

They would leave their house early in the morning and wind over to Main Street to the café where they would order an espresso drink. Then they would window-shop and look at all the new antique items in the windows, things that most people they knew wouldn't buy, but that they coveted: a Victrola, a stained-glass window, a sewing machine. The girls would fill imaginary houses with those antiques, only to lose them to the people who came up from the city for the summer. Those people had money and would rent the pretty houses and borrow boats to motor along the river. They would say they wanted to stay forever, but they always left with no fuss after Labor Day.

Tired of looping Main Street, the girls would head over to Celina's for lunch, arriving in time for summer salad or grilled cheese sandwiches or watermelon slices. And the rest of the day was filled with sun and iced tea and throwing the Frisbee around.

Sometimes Tessa's eyes would linger on the woods, wondering if she would see Jasper again at all that summer, or if she would have to wait for the first day of school. If she waited till then, she was afraid she would ignore him along with everyone else. But she would want to pull at the weird sweater he sported and hide out at the corner undesirable table near the garbage cans and read a strange book with him that no one else would have ever heard of. That is what drew her to him.

"What's that?" Celina asked.

Tessa caught the Frisbee, and saw, in the woods, a glint of something. She threw it to Lulu.

"I don't see anything," she said. But she knew that it was Jasper. He was watching them from the trees. He was wearing brown, blending in, except for his sunglasses, which kept catching the light as he moved his head from side to side, his eyes following the arc of the Frisbee.

"Oh my God," Celina said starting to laugh. "It's that weirdo, Jasper."

Tessa froze. She knew that everyone thought that about him, but while her heart had jumped and thrilled at the sound of his name,

Celina's heart had recoiled. Tessa knew that Jasper was weird, but to hear someone say it out loud made her stumble as she jumped for the disc. She fell to the grass facing the dirt before she rolled onto her back. Celina and Lulu ran to her, not because they were worried that she was hurt, but because they were giggling.

"He's watching us. Do you think he's a pervert?" Celina asked.

"What's a pervert, exactly?" Lulu asked.

"It's like when you watch people and it turns you on and stuff," Celina said.

"Well, maybe I'm a pervert," Lulu said.

"We're definitely perverts, but we're not weirdo perverts like Jasper," Celina said.

"Maybe we should ask him to join us?" Tessa said. Even though they were laughing at him, Tessa wanted to feel his lips on hers again.

"Don't be ridiculous! Jasper Kleine doesn't hang out with anyone. He barely talks!" Celina said. "Besides, I don't want cooties."

"Is there something wrong with him?" Lulu asked.

"He might have been dropped on his head or had measles or something and that affected his social skills," Celina said.

"I think we're too old for cooties," Tessa said. She had kissed him and she hadn't gotten cooties. None of them had had them since elementary school.

"He's still there," Celina said. "I don't want him watching us."

Tessa got up.

"I'll get rid of him," Tessa said. "I'll make him go away."

She walked, making sure that her walk looked normal. She didn't want to run. She didn't want to fly. It seemed like forever, but she finally arrived at the tree that he was leaning against.

"Hey," Jasper said.

"Hey," Tessa said. She was glad her back was to the girls. They couldn't see that she was excited to be standing near him. She fingered the bark on the tree.

"So, you're creeping us out standing over here," Tessa said.

"Do I creep you out?" he asked.

"No," she said.

"That's good," Jasper said.

"Yeah. So, about the staring," Tessa said. "People don't like that."

"Yeah," Jasper said. "I'm not good with people."

"You're good with me," Tessa said.

"You think so?" Jasper said.

Tessa smiled at him.

"Tessa!" Celina was calling her. "Come on!"

"I gotta go," Tessa said. "You should go do something else."

Jasper blinked. He licked his lips. Tessa took her finger and touched his lips.

"Meet me later," he said.

"OK," she said, as she turned to run away from him. She was flushed when she met back up with Celina and Lulu who were now lounging on the patio furniture.

"What did he say?" Celina asked.

"He said sorry," Tessa said. "He won't stand there again."

Then Celina and Lulu changed the subject, but Tessa only heard every sixth word, because her mind was filled with only thoughts of Jasper.

Tessa began kissing Jasper in secret whenever she had the chance, and not one person said that she looked any different. No one teased her that she was in love. No one cooed and cawed as though her first love was as cute as a passel of puppies. No one sighed around her or smiled.

But Tessa *felt* different. She was blooming, too. She could tell it was true when she caught sight of herself in mirrors and windows.

At first she didn't think she liked him at all. She just liked the secret of him. Because whenever Tessa was in a room with Charlie and he cozied up to Lulu, Tessa hurt. She couldn't help but wonder why she wasn't the one that Charlie wanted to be close to all the time, when she always wanted to sit next to him, stare at him, talk to him. But then sometimes, she felt differently about that; and then when she was with Jasper alone in the woods, she couldn't imagine any other eyes than his.

She wasn't sure what real love felt like, but when she lay in the woods with Jasper and they would stare up at the sunlight pouring down through the trees, she would marvel at the powerful thing she felt. It was dark under those trees, but when there was a breeze, the leaves would rustle and the light—when it managed to break through—would stab her and then disappear. It was the same as what she had begun to feel for Jasper; like she'd been stabbed with a sudden light.

Sometimes a deer would come close to them, oblivious that they lay there among the leaves. A twig would crack, and the deer would turn and notice them. Both human and beast would stay very still and stare until after a while, the deer would turn at a noise further along and move elegantly away.

Then they would wrap their arms around each other and pull close. Silence surrounded them. Their breath would fall in time with each other. Their eyes would say everything and their lips would only kiss. Their fingers would find each other and hold fast.

"There's a beast in all of us, you know," Jasper said.

"No," Tessa said.

"Yes, a monster right inside of us all," Jasper said.

They wondered what theirs looked like. They faced each other and blinked while making faces to try to capture the phantom.

Sometimes Jasper and Tessa listened to each other's heart beat or to the river rambling by or to the traffic from the highway a mile away. The sounds were soft, sometimes loud, sometimes like half-understood words. Tessa would turn to Jasper and be amazed by his eyes. She fell into them, they were her secret watering holes, and she would just swim in them. She liked to imagine that he felt the same way about her eyes. He was mostly quiet, though. So she satisfied herself with the fact that they would hold each other tightly, limbs all wrapped up together until she couldn't tell where they were different. Tessa thought that Jasper's skin felt like it was her own skin. And she would cover him in kisses, sometimes confusing her own hand with his.

When Jasper did speak, he wondered aloud.

"Who put that sculpture over by the bridge?"

"What is the purpose of wrapping a string around a ham?"

"Where does the end of the road end?"

"When will I know how old is old?

"How many craters are there on the moon?"

Tessa never knew the answers, but she always tried with all seriousness to answer.

"A small man in a blue peacoat who came down from the mountain ten years ago."

"That is how a pig is caught."

"At the place where the tallest tree and smallest stone meet."

"When you forget where your bicycle is chained."

"Not more than needles on a pine tree, not less than the licks it takes to finish an ice-cream cone."

Jasper would laugh and say that she could be right, but might be wrong. Tessa was sure that it didn't matter. Sometimes she would play an imaginary game with herself where she would try to imagine what it would be like to grow older and find out the right answers together. But older seemed like something so far away that even a year from now seemed like a forever away.

Initially Tessa hated that Lulu was always tagging along. But soon Tessa began to secretly like the fact that Lulu was with them. Lulu being there gave her a chance to slip away by herself. The girls would lie around in Celina's cool bedroom and flip through magazines and paint their nails and talk about kissing. And then Tessa would go to the kitchen or to the bathroom or to get something back home or at the store down the street, and could do so and take her time without leaving either of them alone.

She would disappear from Celina's house and slip into the adjacent woods to meet Jasper. Sometimes they would steal quick kisses, sometimes they would say hello and finish a debate from a topic they had discussed the day before, or they would walk down to Main Street. When they did, they were careful to walk on opposite sides of the street so that they didn't look like they were together. They would go to the convenience store and buy ice-cream sandwiches. They would pretend to ignore each other, but they would lean into the freezer at the same time to reach for the ice cream and their fingers would touch, and despite the cold and the ice, there was always a definite shock of warmth between them.

After taking too long lingering for one last moment with Jasper, Tessa would bring the ice cream, now soft, back to Celina's house. And more often than not, Celina and Lulu hardly even noticed that Tessa had been away for any unusual length of time. They would have decided on some late afternoon or evening plan without her. Sometimes it was boating, sometimes going to the cornfield, sometimes getting one of their parents to drive them to the mall so they could shop or see a movie. Whatever it was, it always involved Charlie and his friends and Tessa always agreed that it was a good plan.

Sometimes Tessa tried to imagine suggesting inviting Jasper to come with them all. She rolled the idea around in her mind more than once. She even asked him if he'd like her to invite him along. He ran his hands through his hair and shook his head.

"No, I don't think so."

Jasper told her that he wasn't interested in laughing stupidly or flinging popcorn or shoplifting chocolate bars from Rite Aid.

"One day you'll want to come," Tessa said.

"Unlikely."

But truthfully, she could never picture it becoming a reality. Jasper seemed so *other*. Although if she had thought about it in a different way, she probably would have realized that she could have maybe convinced him that it was a good idea. That playing normal meant spending more time with Tessa. Jasper would have been happy to do that.

Instead, he watched from his house as they all left without him.

chapter eight

DON'T LOOK AT ME.

I'M NOT AFRAID.

BAM

MAYBE YOU SHOULD BE.

assk if he's sspoken to him.

tell him that you're being ignored.

maybe he can explain it all.

...

HEY—

I HAVE A GAME AFTER SCHOOL TODAY.

YOU SHOULD COME.

HEY!

COME JOIN US!

NO!

chapter nine

Despite their best intentions, there was a friction between the sisters that was undeniable. You could feel it in the house. They sat with it at breakfast. They passed it between them as though it were something simple, like the salt or the bacon or the coffee.

Tessa had tried to suppress the grudge she had about Lulu stealing Charlie. She had kept it inside, pushed down to fill all the crushed cracks about it. Tessa knew that she should maybe let it go. But still, it wasn't fair. Tessa felt strongly that despite the fact that she secretly had Jasper, it didn't matter.

And then sometimes, to make things worse, Lulu would rub it in. It might not have been on purpose, but it felt like it. Lulu would come home and swoon around the living room. Sighing heavily. Touching things on the shelves. She did it on purpose. She would pull out a book and put it back or pick up an object and replace it just so. Some-times, when she sighed she would quietly say the word that Tessa didn't want to hear.

"*Charlie.*"

Tessa tried to let it go.

But every time Tessa looked at Lulu, Tessa's eyes were not soft or open. They stared out at her sister harder than they should have. They were hurtful. They were harsh.

"Don't look at me like that," Lulu said.

"Like what?"

"All mean."

Tessa couldn't help herself. Her eyes were *accusing.* And rightly so. Tessa felt that Lulu had a lot to be sorry for. Lulu had stolen some-thing from Tessa. She wasn't innocent in the affair. She knew why Tessa looked at her that way.

"What should I do?" Lulu said.

"You know," Tessa said.

"I do not," Lulu said. But the look she gave Tessa told her that she did know what would make things right. Lulu could make things better in the house—with a sincere apology.

After all, hadn't Lulu heard all about Charlie from Tessa? Hadn't she even gone with Tessa to football games and cheered him on, never once thinking of him as someone that was for her?

Lulu always said she could barely keep track of which one he was on the field. She could only remember him by his number: Evans 10. And after the games she used to say that she didn't think that Charlie was her type. She liked boys who were soft and dreamy looking, like the ones on the posters in her bedroom. The ones whose fan clubs she'd joined. They had longish hair and full lips and didn't look like they would ever turn into men. They were *safe.*

One night in their shared bathroom, Tessa caught Lulu rubbing cream on her chin.

"What's wrong with your face?" Tessa said.

Lulu nearly burst into tears.

"Is it awful? Do I look awful?" Lulu cried.

"Yes," Tessa said. And that made her feel a little bit better.

"It's just that Charlie is like, a *man!*" Lulu said. "He has the beginnings of a mustache and beard and I can feel it sometimes when he's forgotten to shave. It's so stubbly!"

"That's gross," Tessa said. She looked at her own face in the mirror as she washed it with soap and put her hair band in to keep her curls and their oil off her forehead while she slept. She had no rawness despite having kissed Jasper for an hour that day. Jasper was made up of soft. Soft skin. Soft eyes. Soft lips. Soft mustache.

"It's a prickly little thing, and it makes my mouth and chin raw when we kiss," Lulu said.

Tessa noticed that her sister's lips were shiny with too much Chapstick.

"Tell him to shave," Tessa said.

Lulu threw her hands up in the air.

"I do! And he always promises that he will! But then he forgets, because he doesn't really have that much hair. It's just so pointy! Even after three days he looks clean shaven, but I know he's not because then this happens!"

Tessa felt sorry for her sister and for a moment she softened. She turned to Lulu and listened. Lulu blabbered on. Confiding in Tessa; sharing. It was almost like old times. Except that Tessa didn't say anything back that was helpful or comforting. She was as unyielding as a stone wall.

And it was strange, because they had always shared—always. It was only since the carnival that things had started to change. Sometimes Tessa even wanted to share. Who better to share secrets with than your sister?

It pinched Tessa deep down that she was hurting Lulu. But it couldn't be helped.

One day, after almost enough kisses from Jasper in the woods, Tessa could tell that Lulu knew that something was up. She came around the house and found Lulu and Celina on the front porch sitting on the porch swing. They looked upset.

"Where were you?" Lulu asked.

"Nowhere," Tessa responded. She handed them the melted ice cream.

Lulu put her hands on her hips and pursed her lips in an I-know-better way.

"What?" Tessa challenged.

Then Lulu stood up and plucked a pine needle caught in Tessa's hair. Presented it as evidence.

"I went down to the river," Tessa said. "I went walking in the woods on the way back. It's none of your business."

"We've been waiting for *forever*," Celina said.

"I hardly thought you noticed," Tessa said.

"What is that supposed to mean?" Celina asked.

Tessa slid a look over at Lulu, and without words, Celina softened. She knew, the way that a good friend clues in, sometimes late, but eventually, that she had been paying too much attention to Lulu.

"We're late," Lulu said. "Now the stores will be closed."

Tessa didn't care about the stores.

"We can go tomorrow, Lulu." Celina said.

Lulu was still fingering the pine needle, looking at it with eyes that remembered the stories they used to tell each other about those woods.

Tessa knew that her sister would ask no more questions about it, even if Celina did. After all, didn't Lulu like to walk by herself in those very woods? Didn't she like to imagine that she was the only girl alive on the whole planet? Didn't she, on occasion, sit with her back to a tree and read a book, or do some other thing, like dream, or think. It was quiet in the woods. And day-to-day life was always so noisy: their parents asking all kinds of questions, teachers making demands that facts and numbers be remembered, and friends and social obligations that required immediate attention through IMs, texts, emails, and phone calls. Sometimes, a walk in the woods was the only way to escape.

It was the quiet.

It took Lulu a couple of more days to muster up the courage to do it. But it was as though the fact that Tessa was keeping things from her had made her see things differently. One night, after a day of the silent treatment from Tessa, she took a deep breath and said it aloud.

"I'm sorry," Lulu said. Putting her hand across the dinner table and squeezing her sister's hand. "I'm so sorry for everything."

Immediately Tessa felt lighter. Like the sorriness inside of her had changed its state from a heavy element to a light one. She was not experienced at accepting apologies and was afraid that she would do it clumsily.

"You should be," Tessa said. As soon as the words came out of her mouth, she knew for sure that she had accepted it wrong.

Lulu left the room and slammed the door.

The apology hadn't changed anything.

chapter ten

THIS IS THE PLACE.

THERE IS THE TREE KNOT THAT LOOKS LIKE AN OLD MAN.

THERE IS THE ROOT THAT COULD BE A BRIDGE TO A MAGICAL PLACE.

THERE IS THE STUMP TO PUT COLD DRINKS ON.

I REMEMBER IT ALL.

THE LEAVES LOOK LIKE SNOW.

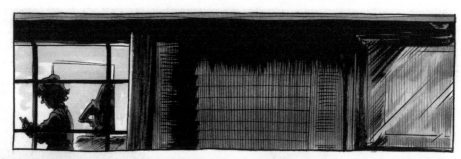

STAR LIGHT,

STAR BRIGHT,

ON THIS STAR I WISH TONIGHT.

I WISH I WAS A **GIRL** AGAIN.

PLEASE MAKE ME A GIRL.

SSSSLEEP.

SSSLEEP.

SSSLEEP.

chapter eleven

Right after Lulu kissed Charlie at the carnival, it was discovered that her feet had grown two sizes. Lulu's mother took them shopping and Lulu got four new pairs of shoes—all of them beautiful. Tessa begged for a new pair, too. But their mother pointed out that now that Tessa had all of Lulu's shoes as well as her own, she had many more shoes than her sister. Tessa would have to settle for the hand-me-downs. Lulu brought all her old shoes and dumped them into Tessa's closet.

Even though they were a little over a year apart, Tessa and Lulu always had been almost the same size. Sometimes one of them had a little spurt and then the other caught up. And then it was the younger sister's turn to grow. But one thing that had always remained the same size was their feet. In the past, they had always been able to share shoes.

"Here," Lulu said. "I don't need these anymore."

This was the beginning of the end. Lulu's feet were bigger than Tessa's, and somehow, in Lulu's size, the shoes were always cuter.

When Lulu grew another two inches, it became clear that Lulu had sprouted and Tessa had leveled off. Lulu gave her older sister all of her cast-off sweaters, skirts, and dresses. Tessa was a smoldering coal ready to light up at any moment. It was confusing to look up at her younger sister. It made her angry sometimes.

Their mother would tell them to go shopping.

"Girls, why don't I drop you off at the mall today and get Lulu some new things?" she'd said. When they got there she'd give Lulu some cash and tell her to spend it wisely.

Tessa would put out her hand for her cash, and her mother would look at her as though she should know better.

"I need new things, too."

"Tessa, we're not made of money," their mother said. "You'll have to make do with what you have. Besides, you'll have all of Lulu's old clothes."

At the mall, Lulu would skip from store to store, trying on everything aided by Celina, who acted as stylist, pulling things that made her look chic.

"You're going to be the best dressed freshman this year," Celina said. "Everyone is going to want to be your friend."

Tessa would finger the things she wanted but couldn't buy. She'd act impatiently and hurry them out of the store. She'd pretend she couldn't find what they were looking for when Lulu and Celina called upon her from the dressing room to find a different size. She'd go to the food court and sit with all the bags while they went to just one more store.

Tessa believed that Lulu was stealing her place. Now Lulu was tall.

Now she was close with Celina. Now she had Charlie. Tessa thought that Lulu was stealing everything that was rightfully hers. Especially the new shoes.

Once, they got to Celina's house before Charlie and the boys came over, and Tessa faked a headache. She didn't want them to see her in her same old clothes. Not while Lulu and Celina were changing into their fresh new outfits and looking like they were closer than ever. How could she enjoy burgers and a movie in her same old clothes? She couldn't.

"Feel better," Celina said.

"See you at home," Lulu said.

If there were such a thing as a dark cloud over someone's head, Tessa had one. It was a stormy little thing. With hail and lightning and thunder. And no silver lining.

Tessa stood in the hallway of Celina's house. It was filled with bookcases and knickknack holders made of modern wood that curved. It looked both old and futuristic at the same time. She felt further away from her best friend and her sister than ever. She thought she would go straight home. But instead, she found herself in the woods on the path to Jasper's house. She imagined that he'd invite her in and she would see his room. Maybe they would watch a movie. Or play his video games. Then before the movie let out, she'd go home and say she'd decided to get some peppermint tea on Main Street.

It was the first time that she'd been to his house. And the sight of it startled her. The porch looked unstable. The roof looked sharp. The windows like eyes. She called his name from the lawn

"Jasper. *Jasper.*"

The door swung open and through the screen Tessa could see the figure of a woman. Her hair was badly in need of a dye job. Her shirt had stains on it.

"Who's there?"

"Is Jasper home?"

"I don't like people coming to the house," the woman said.

"I was next door," Tessa said. "I just wanted to say hello."

"I don't like surprise visits. Next time you should call."

Jasper appeared. He pushed his mother aside and told her it was all right. His mother retreated into the house. Tessa stepped forward.

"No," he said. "I'll come out."

He quickly closed the door and met her on the lawn and then ushered her into the woods.

"What's up?" he said. "Is something wrong?"

Everything was wrong.

She lay in Jasper's arms and cried. She cried and complained about the shoes, about Celina, about her parents, and some more about the shoes. She didn't mention Charlie, although she was crying about him, too. She couldn't say anything about that. Jasper was understanding, but he wouldn't understand about Charlie.

He listened. He clucked. He nodded. He tried to be helpful.

"Can you take her shoes and stuff them with Kleenex?" he asked.

"No," Tessa said.

"Can you wear socks?"

"No."

"Can you talk to your mom? Tell her you need new shoes, too?"

"No."

"Your dad?"

"No."

"There must be something you can do."

"No."

"Well, the shoes you're wearing now look really good. I like them."

Tessa was exasperated. She wondered why he couldn't understand. She cried harder. Jasper pulled her in close and kissed her all over, even her tears.

"Your tears taste sweet even though they are salty," Jasper said.

But Tessa didn't smile. So he made some goofy voices. First a robot. Then a dinosaur. Then a pirate. Then he bellowed like a wild beast.

And then Tessa couldn't help but smile. And smiling led to laughing. And laughing led to feeling better. And then they spread out and read for a while, stealing glances at the birds in the trees and at each other.

When Tessa got home, she noticed Lulu's brand-new cherry colored clogs sitting on the front stoop. The glow of being with Jasper was extinguished. She hated the clogs. Felt green with envy. Tried them on hoping that her feet had somehow grown two sizes since lunchtime.

They hadn't.

She popped four pieces of gum into her mouth and chewed. When the flavor was all gone, she took the enormous wad and stuffed it into the toe of the clog.

The shoes were ruined.

Lulu had to throw them out.

One pair of shoes down. Three more to go.

chapter twelve

COME IN. IT'S GETTING COLD OUTSIDE.

THE WIND'S TURNED.

WELL.

LET'S SEE THEM

YOU'LL TURN TO STONE.

NONSENSE.

YOU THINK I DON'T KNOW HOW TO PROTECT MYSELF?

I PROMISED TO HELP YOU IF YOU **LET** ME HELP YOU.

HOWWWWW

THEY'RE AWAKE AGAIN.

THERE'S NOTHING MORE I CAN DO TODAY.

I DON'T WANT TO COME HERE ANYMORE.

I CAN'T FORCE YOU TO COME HERE.

YOU MUST COME ON YOUR OWN.

THIS IS THE ONLY PLACE WHERE THEY LEAVE ME ALONE.

WELL, THAT'S SOMETHING.

ONE LAST PIECE OF ADVICE.

chapter thirteen

It would have all been fine except for their parents, who meant well, but couldn't possibly understand the silent war that was being waged between the sisters. They only saw that they had two good kids. Two good girls.

Lulu only had a pair of flip-flops left. They were a bit too small. Her heels hung over the backs a little. But she didn't say anything. She didn't complain. Tessa didn't feel badly about ruining all of Lulu's shoes. Small shoes were a little price. Small shoes were better than loneliness. Tessa liked to imagine that Lulu took it as a fair and just punishment. And that each time she kissed Charlie she felt the kiss all the way down to her exposed toes.

After all, hadn't she stolen her crush? After all, didn't Tessa have to pretend to be all alone? Didn't Tessa have to slip off to the woods to get away from all the kissing? Wasn't that why she'd ended up with

Jasper, about whom she couldn't even tell anyone? Her dirty, beautiful secret.

"Lulu, why don't you invite your boyfriend over to dinner this weekend?" their father said at the breakfast table. He seemed pleased with himself.

Their mother nodded in agreement and poured them all some more coffee, her sleeve tattoos seemingly alive as she bent and straightened her wrist.

"No," Lulu said.

"No," Tessa said.

Their father looked over at them both from behind the cup of coffee as it reached his lips and clicked against his lip ring. He took a long sip and put the cup back down on the table. He looked at them again, first to one girl, then to the other.

"Are you embarrassed?" he asked.

"No," Lulu said.

"Does he have horns growing out of his head?" he asked.

"No," Lulu giggled.

"Does he have scales instead of skin?" he asked.

"No," Lulu belly laughed.

"Does he smell terrible? Spit smoke? Shoot lasers out of his eyes?"

The girls were guffawing now. Their father smiled. Their mother sat down and finished her pancakes. The matter was resolved.

"I have to go meet Charlie," Lulu said. "I'll ask him today."

"I'll make a roast chicken," their dad said.

Tessa hated that she couldn't show Jasper off and get the same reaction that Lulu got about her Charlie.

Tessa lay diagonally on Celina's bed watching while Celina experimented with the number of braids she could pile on top of her head. It seemed like they hadn't had a day alone in forever.

"You have to come, Celina," Tessa begged.

"Why?" Celina asked.

Tessa was quiet. She didn't want to have to say it. That she didn't want to be alone.

"Just come, *please.*"

"You're hopeless!"

Celina was so good at switching from one moment to the next. She moved from delighted to annoyed back to giddy with ease. It was Celina's gift to be in the moment and then to let that moment go and move to the next one. For Tessa, things stuck with her. They colored her whole day. But having Celina as a friend made it easier to bear. Celina's mood, when happy, was infectious.

Celina sighed and joined her friend on the bed. She put her arms around her friend and they lay there like they always had since they were little girls. Celina knew just what she needed. Just like the old days. Tessa knew that she could count on Celina no matter what. Celina was Tessa's best friend. Celina was on her side. And best friends always knew when to show up.

"OK," Tessa said. "Your dad's cooking is better than my mom's."

"I hate her. I hate Lulu," Tessa said. She was glad to be able to talk openly with Celina.

"No you don't," Celina said. "She's just your sister."

"You wouldn't know anything about it," Tessa said. "You don't have a sister. They're terrible."

"If I had a sister, I would hate her, too," Celina said with camaraderie.

"You would?"

"Sure," Celina shrugged. Tessa knew that Celina was likely just being nice. But she took it anyway.

"She's pretty," Tessa said.

"You're pretty," Celina said.

"She's smart," Tessa said.

"You're smart," Celina said.

"Charlie likes her," Tessa said.

"Charlie is a boy," Celina said, which in her mind meant that he was dumb. "You two are so alike, like peas in a pod. Like twin suns."

"That's not true," Tessa said. "If we were the same then Charlie would've liked me."

Celina didn't have an answer for that. She just wanted to get to the fun part of the day. Celina gave Tessa a look that said, "I have indulged you enough and now it is getting boring."

Tessa knew deep down that no one could explain why anyone liked anyone else. It was a mystery. Why didn't Tessa like Dylan or Tony or Lionel? Why did she slip off into the woods to be with Jasper, whom nobody liked? It was a mystery.

Even though Charlie wasn't her boyfriend, Tessa was just as nervous as Lulu before he came over. How would her parents look to him? Would he think that her dad's long hair and piercings or her mother's sleeve tattoos were weird? Would her father, not a sports person at all, try to engage Charlie in conversation about things he didn't know about and then look dumb? Would her mother go on and on about her rock tours with her riot grrrl band, bring out her guitar, play a few of the old songs? Would she put on an mp3 of her one college radio hit and hope that he recognized it?

Tessa could see the tension in Lulu as well. She saw when Lulu became flushed, it made her look pretty. Noticed that when her voice tightened up, it became breathy, like an old movie star and when her hands trembled, even Tessa reached out to help her. By the time the doorbell finally rang and she could hear Charlie down in the entrance way, Lulu had to pee again for the fourth time. Tessa wanted to help her sister through it. But instead, she went down to answer the door.

Dinner went smoothly. Her parents didn't embarrass them. They were perfectly pleasant. Charlie was polite; he'd brought flowers and declared that they were for everyone in the house, which had impressed even her. But Tessa cringed with jealousy as she saw Charlie sneak his hand under the table and imagined what their hands were doing under there. Tessa pursed her lips when he complimented every bite he took of dinner. Tessa was quiet but polite and threw only the occasional mean look at Lulu.

Charlie helped their mother make the coffee.

Tessa couldn't understand the way these things worked or why she felt so conflicted. She *had* a boyfriend. She felt that she should be happy, too.

Jasper was likely waiting for her right now with a blanket and a Thermos of hot tea in the woods. She could have asked to leave early, before dessert. She had a boy who liked her. He was right there in the woods. She didn't have to figure out what top to wear, or which lip gloss to apply, or how to do her hair. Jasper just liked her.

But instead she felt as if she wanted to be on the couch whispering with Celina and squeezing herself in between Charlie and Lulu to widen the space between them.

She looked at the time and ignored it.

After dinner they all sat in the living room drinking their coffee.

Lulu and Charlie held hands. Celina talked about Tony. Tessa felt as though she was in a different club than all of them.

And even though no one said it, Tessa felt as if everyone was wondering why no boy had asked her out that summer. Or why she didn't mention anyone special that she had a crush on.

Even though she was older. Even though she was just as good as Lulu. Lulu wasn't everything. Tessa didn't have to be left out of the support that her parents were showing. Lulu could share.

Couldn't she have had a boy here, too? Couldn't Jasper have come over? With his greasy hair? His in-your-face ways? His a little too edgy edge? His all-wrongness could be sitting in this living room. He didn't have to be a secret. He could be here, too.

She wanted to figure out how to get back in the club.

Tessa stood up. Cleared her throat. Told the truth.

"I'm dating Jasper," she said. "He's my boyfriend and we are in love."

Celina didn't mean to laugh. But she did.

"That is so random!" Celina said.

Tessa knew that it was surprising because it seemed so out of left field. But it had been her secret for weeks now, and so it just seemed natural.

"You don't have to make up a boy," Lulu said. Lulu sounded annoyed, as if she thought that Tessa was trying to steal her spotlight.

Charlie looked uncomfortable, as though he were suddenly caught between the wills of girls. Her parents looked at each other and suddenly agreed to clear the table and clean the dishes.

"I'm not lying," Tessa said. "I've been with him since the carnival."

"He's a weirdo," Celina said. "Isn't he? We think he's weird, right?"

"Jasper's OK," Charlie said. "I mean, he's not so bad a guy."

"He's not weird, he's unique," Tessa said.

"Is that where you've been sneaking off to?" Lulu demanded to know.

"I think I'm going to go," Charlie said. He put his coffee cup down but took an extra cookie for his drive home.

"Jasper?" Celina said. "He's greasy."

"He's not," Tessa said. Although really he was. But her chest tightened with feeling for him; his smile, his tender eyes, his fingers touching hers, his breath, his arm around her waist, his fine mind, his big thoughts, his big dreams.

"I don't think I've ever talked to him," Celina said, "even though he's lived next door to me my whole life."

"So, Lulu, I'll see you tomorrow at the movies, right?" Charlie said. His coat was on. He looked a little disappointed that he was not going to have the make out session that he had expected.

"I'll ask Jasper to come with us to the movies tomorrow night," Tessa said.

"Great," Lulu said. "It can be a double date."

"Triple date," Celina said. "I'll go with Tony."

"Great," Charlie said (although it didn't sound as if he meant that).

Charlie kissed Lulu a little self-consciously in front of everyone and left.

"We both have boyfriends," Lulu said. And she had said it like she was relieved.

Everyone knew that if Tessa was with Jasper, Lulu was off the hook about Charlie. The war was over.

"I'll go tell him right now," Tessa pulled on her sweater. Jumped on her bike. Rang the tiny bike bell. Whooped and hollered all the way to the forest. She was determined that she could convince him.

chapter fourteen

HELLO.

HELLO.

THERE'S NO ROOM HERE. I HAVE TO GO ALONE.

I UNDERSTAND.

HOT CHOCOLATE? AFTER?

i don't know...

I'LL WAIT FOR YOU.

♪ oh my darlin, oh my darlin, ♫

♪ oh my daaaarlin clementine ♪

thou art lost and gone forever ♪

dreadful sorry, clementine.

light she was, and like a fairy, and her shoes were number nine,

herring boxes, without topses,

sandals were for clementine. ♪

how ♪ i missed her! how i missed her,

how i missed my clementine. ♪

but i kissed her little sister,

i forgot my clementine.

YOU MADE IT!!

GIFT SHOP

chapter
fifteen

Tessa stood out there on the sidewalk, in front of the
movie box office. The rain was coming down. It was soft, more like a
mist. First she figured that she'd just miss the commercials. Then the
previews. Then the first ten minutes. Then twenty. After thirty minutes of standing there on the sidewalk, all the latecomers had already
straggled in and settled in their seats with hands halfway through
their popcorn.

She knew.

He wasn't coming.

She couldn't believe that he wouldn't come.

He'd promised.

"I promise," he had said.

And then she had reached for him and he'd reached for her and it felt so good to be in his arms and half naked. They weren't just making promises with words, but with their bodies.

She lay back on the blanket that he always had spread on the ground, a childhood comforter, worn down from use, splattered with cowboy themes that bucked beneath her. She was overcome in waves. Was this what bliss was, or pure joy? Complete happiness?

She imagined that it was. She imagined that this moment, frozen, was the one that she would carry with her in her heart forever.

Up above them, the sky was full of stars going about their business of warming up distant planets. A part of their light reached Tessa. She was warm on arms full of promises and potential.

She could just imagine it. He would come and meet her and her friends. They would share a bucket of popcorn, with butter in the middle. They would agree to put M&Ms on the top for salt and sweet goodness. They would hold hands. Charlie and Tony would see that Jasper was all right. Jasper would see that hanging out with the group wasn't so bad. That he wouldn't have to agree with everything they said. That he could disagree and be himself. Be different.

"I promise," he had said. "I promise I'll try."

But now, she was still standing by the box office, holding on to the now-soggy tickets. Ink running. Ruined. She didn't get the refund for the unripped stubs.

She couldn't go in.

She couldn't face her friends.

She shivered in the rain. She looked at the café, went in and sat by the window. Staring every minute outside, Tessa hardly dared to blink in case he had changed his mind.

"Something must have happened," she said aloud to no one in particular. The waitress cleaned the table next to her with a cloth. A man turned the page of his book. A girl typed away furiously at her laptop.

She finally texted Jasper.

"Where are you?"

She texted him again.

"Are you OK?"

She texted him again.

"Did something happen?"

She texted him again.

"You're an asshole."

She texted him again.

"WHERE ARE YOU?"

She texted him again.

"Why?"

She texted him again.

"Meet me. Please meet me."

Tessa checked her phone. There was nothing.

But deep down Tessa knew. It was one world and another colliding. He had told her that planets have to stay in orbit. He could be her moon. But he had to be on his own.

The sidewalk became crowded with people as the movie let out. She saw her friends. She slunk into her chair, hoping that they wouldn't see her and think that she just went off to be alone with Jasper. She didn't want them to think that he stood her up. But Celina turned around and caught sight of her. Tessa didn't want them to come in with their boyfriends when she was sitting alone.

But she didn't have to worry. Celina waved the boys away. Charlie and Tony looked surprised. But then Lulu joined in the shooing them away. The boys shrugged and shuffled down the street and disappeared, and the two girls came in and joined Tessa, ordering a chocolate cupcake for them all to share.

After a long silence Celina spoke.

"You don't have to pretend to have a boyfriend to impress us," Celina said.

"I'm not pretending," Tessa said.

Lulu squeezed her sister's hand warmly, to show support, but to Tessa it felt like a condemnation.

"I'm not a liar," Tessa said.

"I know," Lulu said. But she didn't sound sure.

"Did you try to reach him?" Celina asked.

"Did something happen?" Lulu asked.

"I'm going to walk home," Tessa said.

"But it's dark," Celina said.

"I don't think you should be alone," Lulu said.

"I don't care," Tessa said and her feet, which had been so firmly planted on the sidewalk for two hours were suddenly itching to move out of there. Tessa walked. And walked and walked.

He was there, in the woods, under a makeshift tarp that slapped against the trees. Jasper was sitting there and he looked so different. So slight. So small. So flawed.

Tessa's eyes hardened.

"I can explain," he said.

"How? How can you explain?"

"My mom wanted me to help her."

"Don't blame your mom."

"I'm not. It just made me a little late getting out the door. But I went. I showed up."

Tessa stared at him. Not saying anything. She had been there. She'd been looking for him. She never saw him. She waited for him to continue.

"I went. I went to the movies. I was across the street, and I saw you and your friends. I was going to come and join you. But you all looked the same."

"No we didn't."

"Yes. You did. You all looked like you had some secret uniform. The way your hands moved. The way you and your sister flipped your hair. The way Charlie and Tony had their hands in their pockets."

"So what?"

"I just wanted to hang out with you. I just wanted it to be like it was. Just me and you and not the whole world."

"But we can't just live in these woods!" Tessa said.

"Why not?"

"Because what about when school starts? What about then?"

"Exactly. I don't want to have to sit with you at lunch. I don't want to have to go to this party or that. I just want us to be alone. Private. Just me and you."

"But that's not the way the world works."

"But it's the way my world works."

"I stood there and waited."

"I know. I'm sorry."

"Why didn't you just tell me no?"

"Because I thought I could do it. I thought I could try to be normal so I could be with you."

"What are you afraid of?" Tessa yelled. "Are you chicken?"

"I'm not chicken."

Full of fury, she hooked her thumbs under armpits and made wings and started to cock a doodle doo. She could see that it bothered him. It made her crow louder.

"Shut up," he said.

"Don't you want to be my boyfriend?"

"Yes. I do. I like you. I *really* like you. I just have to do it my way."

Tessa made more chicken noises.

"Don't be like this," he said. "I said I was sorry. Let's just go back to the way it was."

But something had shifted. The tarp slapped against the tree. The branches bent in the wind. The roots from the trees looked more exposed and gnarled.

She looked at him. All the softness in him had shed. Hard jaw. Sharp chin. Set ways.

He shook his head. Disappointed, he stood up and started to walk away.

She let him walk away until she realized that she wanted it to go back to the way it was before, too. But she was too late. He was gone.

She ended up below Jasper's window.

She threw rocks at it.

She called his name.

She screamed at the tree in front of his window.

She begged.

She apologized.

She cursed.

She pleaded.

His mother came out and told her to go home.

Jasper didn't even come to the window to see how wild he'd made her.

chapter
sixteen

I KNOW WHAT IS BEST FOR THIS SCHOOL, AND **THAT** IS FOR PEOPLE TO TREAT YOU AS THOUGH YOU ARE **NORMAL**.

but when i went to the game.

they all turned to stone.

I WOULD HAVE **HEARD** ABOUT THAT.

≡ sigh ≡

chapter seventeen

For three days the skies were black. The rain pounded so hard that the flowers broke, trees split, and havoc was wreaked. On the fourth day there was sun and quiet and a sky that had never been so blue. After being cooped up inside with no escape, everyone in town emerged like animals from winter's sleep to stretch in the summer day.

Lulu and Tessa hopped on their bikes. They went straight to Celina's. Tessa made a concerted effort to not look over to the woods. She stared instead at the river and at the things that floated by.

It was a fine day. They called Charlie who promised he'd be over in a little bit. The girls put on their swimsuits. Tessa psyched herself up for the arrival of Lionel. She decided that she would flirt with him. Even if he was not Charlie, he was, with no contest, the sweetest of all the boys they knew. His dark blue eyes were full of care. His hands were always clean and soft. He was always paying attention and would point out a pothole or a rusty nail for all to avoid.

"The water is rough," Celina's mom said. "Be careful."

The girls put their blankets and towels down on the dock. They took out their slices of melon and ate. They heard the boys whooping and hollering before they saw them as they ran down the hill. Charlie swept Lulu up into his arms and covered her in kisses. At those kisses, Tessa looked over to Jasper's woods. She wondered if he was there.

Lionel was there on the blanket next to her. He pinched her playfully. She responded the way she saw Lulu and Celina respond with their boys. She was tickled. She was coy. She was not at all like herself. She pretended it didn't matter. Even though something felt hollow and wrong. Even though she longed for Jasper. Even though she did nothing about it.

The river rushed by them. They could see debris from the storm. They could see white-capped swirls.

"That storm was fierce," Tessa said.

"The river looks strong," Charlie said.

"Let's jump in and check it out," Celina said. Celina and Charlie jumped. Tony and Lionel jumped. The river sped them up, and they looked small down where they were. They stuck their hands up in the air. They waved.

Come in. Come in.

Come in. Come in.

Their arms were waving. They were so far down the river already. What a thrill!

The sun shone. The light made the river look silver.

"Let's go!" Lulu said.

"Let's go!" Tessa said.

Jumping.

Tessa went first.

Then Lulu jumped right after Tessa.

She jumped right in.

Tessa hit the water. Freezing. Cold. Loud. Surprising. There was a pulling at her legs. She was being pulled swiftly, now the houses blurred by her. She didn't remember the river ever being this fast. She tried to use her arms, but they had never seemed so heavy. Strange. Usually water made her seem light not heavy. A force twirled her, so now she was facing down river. Up river. Down river. The green of the trees was impossible. The pulling made her go under and her nose was filled with water. Now her head was underwater. Now above. Now under. Now gasping, struggling. Not swimming. Just trying to keep her head above water.

Now being scratched. Now losing air.

She could only think of one thing. *Where is the shore? Where is the shore? Why is it so far away?*

Tessa lifted her arms again. Tried to kick her feet. Nothing worked. Swimming just made her go deeper down.

Where am I?

Scared now. Now she was scared.

Underwater. Underwater. Underwater.

Nothing made sense. Fighting the water was exhausting. She was tired. *Sleepy.*

The sun was turning hazy, filtered through the brown river water. Which way was up? Tessa didn't know.

This does not make any sense.

Go to sleep. She heard voices. Voices singing to her to stop fighting. To stop swimming. To stop. Just stop.

They said to her, "You don't have to try so hard. Just let go."

Just float there. Just rest.

Tessa opened her mouth and there was only water and no air. She thought, *The water is so soft.*

The first thing she saw were his eyes. Blue eyes. Jasper's eyes. And they were wet. At first Tessa thought it was from the water. But then she realized that it was from tears.

She tried to talk. She was glad at first to see Jasper. She'd missed him so much, and she wanted to say she was sorry. Wanted to say she wanted things to be like they were before. She tried to lift her hand to touch his face. She wanted to ask him why he was crying. Couldn't. Didn't feel right. Felt weak. Scratched. She lifted her hand. Cupped his face. Smiled, because that was all she could do.

Sirens blared. Got closer.

"Don't move," he said. "Shhh. Don't move."

She was on the ground. Soaking wet and on the ground. Tessa turned her head. Celina was near her laying on the ground. There was blood on her. She was screaming. Charlie was standing up. His letter jacket was over his shoulders but his skin was blue. His bathing trunks shredded. He was shivering. Tony was by a tree. Hands over his face. Lionel was holding him tenderly.

"What's happening?" Tessa said.

She began to shiver.

"She's going into shock," someone said.

Jasper wrapped her up in a towel. He rubbed her arms and legs. She felt warmer. There was something on her mind. A question she couldn't form. Something was missing.

"Where is Lulu?" she asked.

There was silence. The doors slamming. Celina's mother was screaming.

"Where is Lulu?" she asked again.

142

Walkie-talkies crackling. Firemen. Stretchers. Jasper holding her hand.

"Where is Lulu?" Now panicked. Now remembering how strong the water was. How it was not gentle, as it had been before. How the water had had its way with her. Had tried to beat her and made her slip under it over and over again. How it had pulled her faster than she had wanted to go.

"WHERE IS LULU?"

"LULU!"

"LULU!"

"LULU!"

Jasper hands cupped her hands. His forehead to her forehead.

"I couldn't find her."

"She was with me in the water."

"We couldn't find her."

"She was right next to me in the water."

"I only saw you. I only found you."

And then he blinked. Those blue eyes looking at her.

And she looked back at him with all the parts in her that had been dragged under the water. The part that had her heart. The part that took Lulu. She looked at him and she didn't have to use her words to tell Jasper that she wasn't sorry anymore. That she didn't want him in the woods, she only wanted Lulu out of the water.

The only thing she told him with her eyes was that she hated him.

But she hated herself more for still being alive.

chapter eighteen

SKRITCH
SKRIT

SKRIT

SKRIT

SKRITCH

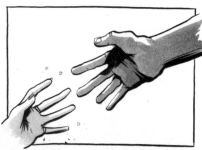

KRAK

CREAK

WAIT!

chapter nineteen

Tessa didn't know that the most beautiful day of summer could be so dark. Even though the sun was out. Even though the sky was a shocking blue. Even though every flower had suddenly decided to bloom again. She wore black. Everyone wore black. Celina wasn't there. She was in the hospital with a broken back. Her back broken. She would never walk again. And Lulu was laid out for all to see before she would be cremated and put in an urn.

It didn't help that there were so many dragonflies and that some-one once told her that dragonflies were the souls of the newly de-parted. Tessa didn't believe that anything magical existed. If there was, then why would Lulu be dead? Why would she be alive?

Her mother was leaning against her father. He was holding her up. Tessa thought that she might sink to her knees and tear at the grass on the ground until it was all gone. She felt a rumbling inside her.

Like there was the mouth of a monster in her belly waiting to swallow her up.

She listened as people said things about Lulu. She spoke words she didn't remember writing. She sang along with the others to a song that Lulu used to listen to on repeat. She watched as they all walked back to their cars. She watched as they went back home and ate food and talked in hushed voices. She watched as they all left, no one really knowing what to say. Her mother in the living room, trying to find some music that would get her through the night. Her father cooking, because that was all he could think of to do.

Tessa had to let them know which outfit Lulu would have wanted to wear. Tessa knew. They wanted to dress her in the wrong dress. She made her mother buy Lulu a pair of shoes. She didn't want her sister in the open casket wearing bedazzled flip flops.

When they finally found Lulu she was bloated and blue. Her bathing suit was shredded. She was not recognizable.

At night Tessa had to cover her ears and pretend that she did not hear her mother wailing. Her mother didn't even sound human anymore. And despite how sad she was, Tessa couldn't help but wonder if her mother would have wailed as loudly for her. Would it have been the same if she had died? Would it have been different?

In the hospital, Celina's face was swollen and her eyes black and blue. Her legs and back wrapped in plaster.

"I'll never walk again," Celina said. "I'll never walk. I just wish I had died."

Tessa ran out of the room.

And where was Jasper?

He had disappeared. Hadn't come to the funeral. Didn't come to hold Tessa's hand. Didn't come to make sure that she was OK.

Charlie did. Charlie came and visited every day. He held her hand.

He read to her from magazines and made her playlists and loaded them up for her. He paid her the kind of attention that she'd always craved and didn't want anymore. After all of that, she realized that she didn't like Charlie. He wasn't for her. He was for Lulu. She wanted Jasper.

Tessa hated the water. Didn't want to shower. Didn't want to drink it. She didn't look out at the river anymore. She couldn't stand the sight of it. She stifled out the sound with loud music and she blasted it upstairs in her room. Her mother was in the garage with her old guitar amp turned up to ten. Mournful fuzz and feedback was mimicking and covering up sobs.

Tessa had lost so much weight in such a short time. She could see the bones of her skeleton pressing through her skin. Paper skin. Blue veins. She thought they might just burst through. She already felt like she had no skin on. She wondered if her bones could just walk away from her, leaving her a puddle of skin on the floor.

That's what she was. They all were puddles of skin.

One night, the stars were out. There was no moon. The night was cruel when it had no moon. Tessa looked out her window. She'd been sitting in the sun nook for hours and had watched the sky go from blue to pink to orange to black. She had seen the first star come out and had made a wish. She sat so long that she saw the constellations come and go.

She had found the blade in the back of her vanity. It was an old one, and it was wrapped in wax paper with a little piece of folded cardboard over it. She'd found it a few years back but only remembered that it was there that night. She opened the drawer, pulled it out all the way. Shook out its contents on the floor: lip liner, pencil sharpener, paper clip, postage stamp, blush brush. There it was. Right there.

Remove the cardboard. Press the point on her thumb. She felt it. Sharp.

She turned her wrist over and wondered which way she should cut. Wondered if she did, if it would hurt? Wondered how long it would take. Wondered if her death would be the same as Lulu's? How much blood would there be? And would it feel like drowning?

At the hospital, Charlie had told her everything, because he had seen it. She could tell that he didn't want to relive it as he told her.

"You were dead," Charlie said after finishing up a sandwich and prompting her to spoon soup into her mouth.

"No, I didn't die," Tessa said. "I *lived*."

He put the spoon down and pressed a hand to his eyes as if it would be easier to talk about if he didn't have to see. He said the words like they didn't belong to him. His other fist punching his thigh marking each event, like bullet points.

"You came out of the water. Jasper pulled you out of the water. And you were so blue. Jasper was screaming that you were blue."

She had been cold when she woke up.

"I don't remember that," Tessa said.

"Jasper punched your chest. Punched it," Charlie said. Charlie was crying, but didn't care that he was. Snot was coming out of his nose and he wiped it with the back of his sleeve. His eyes were still closed.

She had remembered Jasper kissing her. His voice sounded far away. She was floating and he was warm on her lips. And then there was air in her lungs.

"He brought you back," Charlie said. "We thought we'd lost you, too. If it weren't for Jasper . . ."

"But he should have looked for Lulu. He should have gone after her. You all should have."

"We couldn't see her anymore. We only saw you. You are the one that we saw."

Tessa pushed aside the memory of those troubled first days at the hospital.

Tessa put the point of the blade to her wrist. Sweat gathered on her upper lip. Would it hurt? Would someone pull it out of her skin? Wasn't she still drowning now?

She turned her arm over and carved five letters into it: I DIED. There was blood. She sopped it up with Kleenex. She had so many boxes of Kleenex in her room now, mostly empty. The garbage can was full of used ones, and her face was raw from tears.

Tessa came downstairs holding a towel soaked in blood to her wrist. Her mother had screamed when she saw the blood. Then her mother had sunk down to the floor.

"No. No! NO!" She'd said, not seeing at first that Tessa wasn't dead, too.

Her mother collapsed into her father's arms.

"She's OK," he soothed. "She just cut herself."

"Tessa!" her mother screamed. "Tessa. You scared me."

Tessa couldn't look her mother in the eyes. She couldn't say anything to them. She had no words. She couldn't say that she was sorry. If she did, she might break.

Her father told her to go upstairs to bed.

The cuts hurt. They stopped bleeding. She shut the blinds, lay down on the bed and closed her eyes.

When she woke up, there was something different about her. Her head was squirming. She ran to the mirror. Her hair was untamable. It was dreaded. No. Her hair writhed. It was full of snakes.

Tessa ran downstairs. Frightened.

"Mom! Dad!" She was screaming. Her arm was still bleeding. "Mom! Dad!"

She ran into the living room first.

The kitchen second.

They couldn't help her. When they saw her, they turned to stone.

Tessa sat on the first stair and wept.

"I've killed us all," she thought.

chapter
twenty

chapter twenty-one

Alarm clocks always rang too early. They buzzed and buzzed, the loud chime shaking away the safety of sleep or the bliss of a dream. Tessa had hit the snooze button more often than she should have. She would be late. She didn't care about that. She didn't want to go at all.

She was cold and her hair was a mess. She hadn't brushed it since she had come out of the water and the curls had come together to form thick dreads. She touched her feet to the floor and recoiled. She felt around for her slippers. She felt so heavy.

She rummaged through all of her clothes, there were piles of them and she could not find a single thing to wear. She pulled on a pair of dark skinny jeans and a T-shirt. Knowing that she was too skinny to keep warm she found a sweater and pushed the sleeves up. The scab was still there. Perfectly readable now: *I died.*

Tessa could smell breakfast downstairs. They were trying to tempt her to eat. They were always doing that, though they hardly ate themselves. Tessa had no desire to eat anymore. Foods looked foreign to her. She thought of the things on a plate as fuel. If she managed one or two bites, it was OK.

"Think, Tessa, think," she said out loud.

Remembered a wrist cuff. Slipped one on. It covered most of the scar. All you could see was the I. It looked like a cat scratch.

She padded down the stairs quietly.

Her mother was in the living room, her jeans hanging loose off her hips. Her sleeve tattoos lacking in color. She was putting a CD in the player. She couldn't stand to hear the news anymore.

"Too much sadness in the world," her mother said as she turned up the volume on a CD of a band from her youth that she'd rediscovered.

Tessa left her mother in the living room, swaying to the sound of crunchy guitars and jangly melodies. Her mother's hand slapping the beat against her thigh. Eyes closed. Music was surely going to bring the color back. There was always comfort in music.

"I'm making a salad for your lunch," her dad said. He tried to sound chipper. His long hair was brushed and his clean-looking shirt made him seem pulled together. His piercings were extra shiny as though newly polished. But it was all an act. The hair was dirty. The shirt was likely unwashed as well. He scooped salad into a Tupperware container for Tessa.

"First day of school," Tessa said.

"First day," her dad said.

He looked as though he wanted to say something else. His eyes glanced at the wrist cuff. He didn't say anything about it. But she could see his eyes had gotten watery. He looked to the side, avoiding Tessa's gaze. She knew if he said anything else, he would likely cry.

He couldn't cry. He had let Tessa and her mother be as sad as they wanted to be and when they were done, he would take his turn. But right now, he had to be the strong one. Tessa counted on that.

"Maybe I should be homeschooled," Tessa said. "Maybe I should stay here for this semester. After all, everyone else has been there for two months already."

"We talked about this in counseling, Tessa. You've got to go back to school," her dad said. "We all have to get a routine right now."

Tessa traced the pattern on the 1950s table. She drank the coffee that her father placed in front of her.

"Oh, Tessa," her mother said, entering the kitchen. "Your hair."

Her mother came over and tried to smooth the curls, but Tessa knew that it was no good. From weeks of neglect, the hair had curled and dreaded. It would have to be cut off if she ever wanted to comb it again. Right now it was half dreads, and it looked terrible.

"Go get a scarf, and cover it for today," her mother said. "I can cut it later. Or we could go get our hair done." She said it as though it would be a fun thing to do but they both knew that it wouldn't be fun at all.

"No," Tessa said. "It's fine."

Tessa knew where there were cool scarves. They weren't in her room. They were in Lulu's.

"It looks terrible," her mother said. "You look like a mess."

Tessa wanted to say that she was a mess. That her sister had died. That she couldn't bear being alive. She couldn't think about going to school. She didn't care about her hair.

"A scarf would really help, Tessa," her dad gently nudged her.

"Can you go get one?" Tessa asked. "Can you go get one for me?"

Her mother sipped her coffee. Her father snapped the Tupperware bowl shut. No one wanted to go.

"You have to go do it yourself."

Tessa went upstairs. She ran down the hall and went into Lulu's unchanged, still messy room and grabbed a scarf from the top drawer. She didn't care what color it was, or what kind. She just needed it to cover her hair. She tried to ignore the bedazzled flip-flops and the dust on the dollhouse.

Tessa flew back down the stairs. She had to leave now or she would never do it. She would never, ever go.

"Goodbye," she said. "I'm going."

The door slammed behind her.

She walked to school. She hadn't missed the bus, but she wanted to postpone seeing anyone until the last possible moment.

The school looked bigger than she remembered it ever being. She could hear conversations stop mid-sentence as she passed. People whispered.

Across the way she could see the parking lot and Celina being taken out of the new car her parents had bought, which had room enough for a wheelchair. Celina shook Charlie off as he tried to push her up the handicap ramp. Celina would do it herself. Tessa watched as people reached out, ready to help if she needed it. Tessa looked away. Celina was back, too.

"Tessa," Charlie said.

He was standing next to her. Looking sheepish. Or anguished. She couldn't remember what she ever thought was good looking about him. He was like a brother now.

"I'll walk you to class," he said.

"I can't do this," Tessa said.

"Sure you can," he said. "I've got a game after school. Promise me you'll come."

Out of the corner of her eye, she thought she saw Jasper across the street, ditching school already. She wanted to talk to him—or something. He was gone when she looked again.

The bell rang.

So many classes, she moved from one to another as though she were asleep. All of the words that everyone said to her, all of them kind, sounded like nonsense. What did "I'm so sorry for your loss" even mean?

How could they be sorry?

What did they know about loss?

Although every once in a while, someone would say it in such a way that made it seem as if they did know a little about it.

She went to Charlie's football game. When she got there, she saw Celina sitting down with the cheerleaders, who had given her pom-poms that lay in her lap. Celina waved them every once in a while, trying to muster up some spirit. But she was unable to stand up out of her chair to cheer.

Tessa froze. And then, when everyone noticed her just standing there, not coming into the bleachers and not leaving, the eyes on her were unbearable. They burned. She thought she saw Jasper, but it was just wishful thinking.

She ran to the woods. Sat by a tree. Cried. She wanted to be alone, but it was time for therapy.

"You should try to participate," the doctor said. "Try a little bit every day. One small thing."

The doctor was stupid. Treatment wasn't working. Neither were the pills.

She went home to the same darkness. The same sadness. The same mourning.

The phone rang all the time. Someone was always checking in. Tessa never answered the phone anymore. She didn't want to answer the questions. "How are you holding up?"

Terrible. She wanted to say. *I am holding up terribly. I will never be the same.*

Was her sister, Lulu, the luckier one? On the easier path? Was Tessa taking the harder path of life? Everything hurt. Life hurt.

Her head crawled.

"Tessa." Her mother knocked on her bedroom door. "It's Celina."

"I don't want to talk to her," Tessa said.

"Tessa," her mother said. "Can you try? We're all trying."

"I cannot," Tessa said.

Her mother stepped out of the room. Tessa could hear her murmur some excuse to Celina. Even though she didn't need an excuse. Grief was excuse enough.

She knocked again.

"What?" Tessa said. She snapped sometimes. Screamed. Or punched. She didn't know how to behave well anymore. She didn't care.

"Please don't yell at me," her mother asked. She sounded more and more tired all the time. "Celina said that she and Charlie are going to the hayride and corn maze this weekend. They want you to go."

Tessa flopped down on her bed and pulled the pillow over her head. Why didn't they just leave her alone? She didn't want them to keep checking on her or waving at her between classes or trying to get her to sit with them at lunch or be sweet. She wanted Jasper. She wanted Jasper. She wanted Jasper.

No. She wanted *Lulu.*

Why had she lost both of them? Couldn't she have at least kept one of them? And since she couldn't, why not just lose it all?

The principal called her into his office after a week back to check in.

"We know you've had it tough, and we're here to help you," the principal said. He was trying to be nice. He knew that she was likely going to fail this term, and he was trying to tell her that they would give her some leeway. But he told her that her hair was unacceptable.

She hadn't cut it off. Instead she'd dreaded her curls.

"If I cut them off, I'll die!" she screamed. She banged her fists on the table. Violent. The principal jumped back in his chair. Frightened. White.

Tessa ran out of the office.

She didn't mean to erupt, but she was unable to stop feeling so much. Too much. She wanted everyone to feel everything as loudly as she did, too.

He was old. Maybe she'd scared him so badly that his heart had stopped.

That is what she felt like. Like her heart had stopped.

Charlie wouldn't stop trying. He followed her around or found her between every class.

"We're going to the hayride. Will you meet us?" Charlie asked.

She looked at him and said nothing.

Why did everyone think that she could do normal things? She clearly couldn't.

He shouted after her as she walked away. They'd already bought her a ticket. If she changed her mind, it would be waiting.

She smelled it as soon as she walked out of the doctor's office. It was the fall festival. It reminded her of the carnival. Of the movie where Jasper didn't show up. Of before. She didn't know why she bothered to go to the shrink. She was an old witch who knew nothing.

The only thing soothing about her was the dog that lay at her feet. Tessa would pet and stroke the dog during sessions where she mostly said nothing. Sometimes she would hug that dog and bury her face into his fur and just cry. The doctor would say nothing. Or she would ask Tessa to draw pictures. Or she might make some hot chamomile tea and let Tessa cry for a whole hour.

Tessa felt a pang in her stomach. For the first time in months she was hungry. It wasn't the corn. It was the idea of butter. She wanted the taste of salt in her mouth. She left the therapist's and made her way across the mud and stood in line at the corn cart. The vendor wore an orange apron. She bought a corn on the cob. Bit into it. Butter dripped. It was the first delicious thing she'd tasted in months. It was the first thing that had had any flavor at all.

She wandered over to look at the horses and the wagons. Charlie was helping Celina into the first one. Kids were lined up waving their tickets. She turned away, wanting to get out of there, but then she saw him. Jasper. He was in line to get on a wagon.

She tried to wave.

"Do you have a ticket?" the wagon master said. "No ride without a ticket."

Tessa didn't have a ticket.

"I don't have one," she said, suddenly wanting one more than anything. The wagons started to leave. The last one was almost filled up. One of the organizers had come over to the wagon master and whispered something into his ear.

They both looked at Tessa.

"Young lady," he said, and waved over to her. "It's all settled. I'm sorry for the misunderstanding."

He helped her up into the last wagon.

She didn't know anyone in the wagon with her. They were all

much younger than she was. So they didn't look at her strangely. They looked at her as though she were a girl. A girl just like anyone else. A girl that nothing had happened to. They sang songs.

Tessa didn't. She just felt the rhythm of the wheels; the rocking and the rolling and the sweet smell of the hay. She turned her face up to the weakening sun.

The wagon arrived and they all piled out, running into the maze. People were laughing and screaming with joy trying to find their way out again.

Tessa stood at the entrance. She wanted to be excited like she knew she used to be at fall festivals. But her heart would not quicken. She would not let it expand farther than the cage she'd put around it.

"You love this, Tessa," she said to herself. "You love this."

She stepped into the maze, but still she felt nothing. And then she caught a glimpse of someone turning a corner in front of her.

Jasper.

She picked up her pace. Her heart thawing in that way that hurts when one goes from cold to warm too quickly. She kept seeing Jasper as he turned corner after corner right in front of her. She'd lost track of where she was. And then she caught up with him in the middle.

"Jasper," she said. "Jasper."

"Don't," he said and took one step back from her.

"Jasper," Tessa said. And then she realized she didn't know what to say. No words came.

"I'm leaving town," he said. "I guess I should tell you that. I'm going to boarding school next semester."

She wanted to ask him if he'd meet her down by the woods. If they could lay in each other's arms and kiss and sigh. She wondered if they could go back to the way it was before.

"Will I ever see you again?" she asked.

"I don't know," Jasper said.

"I died, too." Tessa said.

"I know," Jasper said. He was blinking hard. His cheeks were flushed.

"Will you ever talk to me again?" Tessa asked.

"That look in your eyes," Jasper said. "That look you gave me when you came back."

"Yes?" Tessa asked. "Yes?"

"I never want to see that look again."

Tessa shifted her weight. Heard the laughing strangers. Felt the crisp wind hinting at the coming winter. Tried to calm her hammering heart.

"I'm sorry," he said. "I'm sorry." He turned to go.

"What kind of look was it?" she called after him.

"Pure hate," Jasper said.

He disappeared down the maze. Tessa waited a heartbeat before she moved. She was sorrier than she'd ever been in her life. She was sorry for her hard eyes. For Jasper's secret heart that she'd mishandled. For ruining all of those shoes.

She swore. She swore again. She swore a third time.

Charlie and Celina were waiting for her when she emerged from the maze. They were there. They were waiting. Tessa knew that she was made up of all kinds of darkness, but Celina and Charlie were the parts inside of her that she could still feel. She would not ever be careless with precious things again.

"Do you want to ride with us?" Celina asked.

"Yes," Tessa said.

"Are you OK?" Celina asked.

"Maybe," Tessa said.

There was still sweetness in the air. She had to stand on her tippy toes to feel it. She could do it. She would. But it was a stretch. There was light up there.

Perhaps she would grow a little taller, and in a year or two it would be easier. She wouldn't have to stretch so far to find the light. It would just be there for her. Waiting. Just like her friends had been.

She took Charlie's hand as he helped her up into the wagon and then climbed in after them.

Cecil Castellucci is a two-time Mac-Dowell Colony fellow, the young adult and children's book editor of the *Los Angeles Review of Books*, and an award-winning author of five books for young adults including *Boy Proof*, *The Plain Janes*, and *Beige*. Her books have been on the ALA Best Books for Young Adults, Quick Picks for Reluctant Readers, Great Graphic Novels for Teens, Amelia Bloomer, and NYPL Books for the Teen Age lists. Cecil lives in Los Angeles, California.

Nate Powell is the author and illustrator of the graphic novel *Swallow Me Whole*, which was a *Los Angeles Times* Book Prize finalist, the 2009 Eisner Award winner for Best Graphic Novel, and an Ignatz Award winner. Nate lives in Bloomington, Indiana.